Grace of an Angel

Story of a computer scientist, his visions, his trials, and the angels around him

ᙅᙚ ᙅᙚ ᙅᙚ

A Christian Tech Romance Novel

Francis Leung

UNDERCOVER
ANGELS
PUBLISHING

San Francisco Bay Area, California

Grace of an Angel

© 2025 by Francis Leung

Published by **Undercover Angels Publishing**
San Francisco Bay Area, California

ISBN 979-8-9936455-0-6

Cover design and publisher mark © Undercover Angels Publishing
Printed in the United States of America
First Edition — December 2025

ᔰ Dedication ᔱ

For those who believe that love and faith
can heal even the deepest wounds.

For one whose presence once taught me
that grace can live even in goodbye.

For those who believed when I doubted —
and for the angels who walk quietly among us.

ᔰ

To my Kelsi —
you may not have wealth,
but you have everything I need in my life —
your grace, your prayers, and your love.

To my Tiffany —
you bring healings to the body,
and let Our Lord give healings to the soul.

To my Daniel —
you shine sunlight into our lives,
and light up the whole world around you.

To my Colin —
you may not have saved my life,
but you've shared the journey, the purpose,
and the brotherhood that made it whole.

To my Jalen and Sabrina —
half a century of friendship turns into a lifetime of fellowship.
Defying distance, thank you for walking each step with me.

❧ Acknowledgments ☙

My heartfelt thanks to my friend, Professor Alvin. Your generous Foreword gave this book its first voice and offered a wisdom far deeper than anything I could have asked for. You noticed things that even I, as the writer, did not fully recognize while I was writing.

To my sister Rachel— you have walked with me through every stage of life: from childhood confidante to the one who believed in my work long before I understood it myself. When I need a sister, you're staying right behind... you know my story. Now I give you my ideal version.

To my family and friends, whose steady encouragement sustained me through every chapter and every late-night revision — thank you for believing in this journey long before it became a book.

To the members of my church fellowship — thank you for your prayers, your patience, and for reminding me that grace often arrives through community.

To the real people whose kindness and friendship inspired many of these characters—you are the unseen angels behind this story.

Above all, I thank my Lord, whose mercy and wisdom guided my heart more surely than any outline or plan. Without His grace, there would be no *Grace of an Angel*.

ॐ

A brilliant researcher designs a device to restore sight and movement, believing technology can heal what faith cannot. But when his own invention fails to save him, he discovers that the truest healing comes not from perfection, but from grace.

Grace of an Angel follows a journey where science meets spirit, and an imperfect invention becomes the vessel of something far greater — a reminder that sometimes, the miracle isn't in what we create, but in what we're given.

ॐ

❧ Table of Contents ❧

ᔰ **Foreword :** *the Gift of Grace* ᔰ

I've spent most of my life writing academic books and teaching sociology—analyzing how people relate to one another and how belief shapes behavior. But when it comes to novels, it's been decades since I last read one. In high school, I could lose myself in a story for hours, turning page after page long after midnight. Later, life, work, and family responsibilities left little room for that kind of escape.

So when my friend Francis, the leader of my fellowship group at church, handed me his manuscript and asked me to write a preface, I didn't quite know what to expect. A retired engineer with no background in literature—he wrote a novel? My curiosity got the better of me. I promised to read a few pages, and a few pages turned into an all-night reading session.

To my surprise, *Grace of an Angel* pulled me in from the start. It reminded me of the quiet joy I once found in fiction, and of the way a good story can illuminate truths that sociology alone cannot capture. Walking my usual 10,000 steps the next morning, I found myself still thinking about its characters and what they revealed about love, purpose, and healing.

What struck me most about *Grace of an Angel* is how naturally it weaves together three strands rarely joined so seamlessly: romance, technology, and faith. At its center is the invention of the "Eyes of an Angel," a breakthrough that uses AI to help the blind walk independently, the paralyzed move again, and stroke patients regain their voices and strength. Yet the novel doesn't celebrate this as a mere triumph of science—it roots it in compassion, human connection, and spiritual purpose.

As someone who is not a Christian, I was especially moved by how faith is portrayed in this book. It is not preached; it is lived. Fraser, the inventor, doesn't see his intelligence as self-made glory but as a gift entrusted to him. His faith grows through people — through love, disappointment, and forgiveness — much as meaning emerges in any human community. This, to me, is where the story finds its moral strength.

And the characters—Fraser and Kelsi, Sarah and Jordan, Britney and Dillon, Summer and Colin—linger in the mind long after the final page. They aren't just names on a page, but people who feel alive, with emotions and struggles we can relate to. They are not perfect heroes but human beings we recognize: uncertain, flawed, hopeful, capable of grace. The coma storyline in particular left a strong impression on me. Not only does it build real tension; it also captures how healing often comes not only through science but through patience, sacrifice, and the mysterious persistence of love.

When I asked Francis whether these characters were drawn from people he knew or from pure imagination, he just looked at me and smiled.

In the end, *Grace of an Angel* is more than a novel about invention or faith. It is a story about seeing—seeing others with compassion, seeing oneself with honesty, and seeing life as a web of relationships where intellect and emotion, science and spirit, reason and faith coexist rather than compete.

For me, it rekindled both the pleasure of reading and the curiosity that first drew me into sociology—the study of what makes us human. I finished the book feeling grateful, thoughtful, and quietly uplifted. I truly enjoyed it, and I believe you will too.

— Alvin Y. So, Ph.D.
Professor Emeritus, HKUST

🙌 Reflection : *from a Sister's Heart* 🙌

Some years ago, quite unexpectedly, I began receiving a stream of reflective essays Francis had written about life since settling in California after college.

Growing up close in age, we had been playmates and confidantes. Blessed with an aptitude for mathematics and physics, his dream had always been to become an engineer and scientist. Those aspirations were fulfilled as he built a successful engineering career, started a family, and took on a spiritual leadership role within his church community.

As I read through his essays, I was struck not only by how clearly he could articulate his thoughts, but also by his willingness to share the triumphs and trials of his work and personal interactions. I never imagined my engineer brother could also be such a fine writer.

After the essays came the early manuscripts—pages of a story he intended to expand into a novel. Those pages kept me mesmerized. The characters felt familiar and deeply human, reminding me of friends and experiences I could relate to. I saw ambition, humility, failure, compassion, and hope—the emotions we all live through.

And unlike the occasional sour notes in some of his earlier essays, this story was told without bitterness.

As his sister, it has been gratifying to see Francis transform his reflections into grace through storytelling.

With the release of this novel, your characters are now ready to meet a broader audience.

Bravo, dear brother—your literary dream has set on sail. Your time has come to shine.

—Rachel M. Leung
Resident, Evanston, Illinois
Retired Finance and Strategy Manager
University of Wisconsin, BBA
Cornell University, MBA

᮷ Preface ᮤ

The idea for *Grace of an Angel* began years ago when I read that scientists were training a monkey to play video games using artificial intelligence.

The news left me wondering—if AI can teach a monkey to play, could it one day help people heal?

That question stayed with me and grew into a story about the meeting point of technology, compassion, and faith. It became a journey of discovery—not just for its characters, but for me as well. It taught me that science can open the eyes, but only grace can open the heart.

Grace of an Angel follows a young researcher whose creation—the **Eyes of an Angel**—was born first from ambition but made whole through compassion. What began as a device to help others see and move again became something far greater: a bridge between science and the soul.

Fraser's brilliance is not measured only in discovery, but in the humility that lets faith shape his reason. His mind designs what his heart dares to believe possible.

Through *Eyes of an Angel*, Katie and Charlie find new life, and later Patrick recovers his voice and strength. Even when Fraser himself faces death, his invention—as small as a wedding ring—becomes his salvation—imperfect in form, yet completed by the tears of the women who love him.

The characters and events are fictional, but the emotions that drive them are drawn from real life—moments of failure, hope, and second chances that I've witnessed or lived myself.

I've learned that miracles do not oppose science—they work through it. They remind us that intellect without compassion is incomplete, and faith without action remains a dream. When the two meet—when brilliance listens to the heart—healing becomes possible.

If this story leads you to see wonder in both creation and Creator, then grace has already done its quiet work again.

— *Francis*

Chapter 1 *The Christmas Illusion*

Magic or Technology?

∽ ∽ ∽

In the computer lab of **U.C. Berkeley**, a young man wearing a funny-looking bike helmet attached to a pair of thick goggles is busy typing at his computer.

Then he switches his screen to a tennis match. He stands up, picks up a tennis racket, and swings as he watches Rafael Nadal return a blistering serve.

Then his phone rings.

"When are you going to pick me up?" a girl's voice comes through.

"In half an hour," the man replies.

After he hangs up, he switches his screen to an art competition. He watches an artist sketching a portrait in close-up, studying every stroke attentively.

Finally, he closes his laptop, puts everything into his backpack, and steps out.

— ✦ —

Over two hundred people fill the church auditorium. Fraser walks slowly onto the stage, standing next to a piano. He sets down his backpack, turns around, and looks at his audience.

It's Christmas time, and Tri-City Church is holding a celebration event. After the choir and a short skit, the highlight of the evening begins — a magic show. Fraser leads a cell group at the church while pursuing his PhD in AI development at UC Berkeley. Known within the church community for his computer expertise and communication skills, he isn't recognized for performing magic or playing musical instruments. His decision to lead a magic show comes as a surprise to all his friends.

"Good evening, brothers and sisters. May the Lord's peace be always with you," Fraser says as he picks up the microphone. "You're probably wondering why I'm up here. I can't sing, I can't dance, and I can't play guitar or piano. If I attempt any of these, you'd all leave in real time!" Even on stage, Fraser carries himself more as a friend than a performer, his humor breaking down the distance between him and the crowd.

As the audience laughs, he steps to the front of the stage and asks, "I need a volunteer who can play piano really well. Anybody?"

A girl sitting in the front row immediately raises her hand. "Fraser, let me be your assistant. You know I can play!"

"Hey Kelsi, of course you play well. But I need someone who doesn't know me for this act, and most people know you're my friend..." Fraser looks at her with a smile and then turns his gaze further into the audience.

"How about you in the third row on the left side? Can you come up here?" He waves to a girl with her hand up, sitting next to an elderly couple. The girl starts walking onto the stage.

"Here he goes again! Always looking for chances to meet pretty girls!" Kelsi mumbles to herself. She's a graduate student at UC Berkeley, pursuing an MBA. She met Fraser in the cafeteria six months ago when he placed his tray across from her table and introduced himself. Since then, they have become good friends, gone on quite a few dates, and she even attends church with him. Although she isn't a Christian, she likes him — probably more than she's willing to admit.

Back on the stage, Fraser addresses the girl. "Seems you come to worship quite often, but we haven't met. I'm Fraser. What's your name?"

"I'm Sarah. My parents and I come every Sunday for the first worship. We're leaving as you're coming in," the girl replies with a friendly smile. "Now, what would you like me to do?"

Down below the stage, Kelsi shifts uncomfortably as she watches Sarah smile at Fraser. Sarah is undeniably pretty. Jealousy is new to her; she's surprised that one smile from

3

Sarah could stir such a storm inside. Fraser has mentioned he'll be performing an act but hasn't explained what it will be. Now he picks a pretty girl as his assistant. She wishes she is the one on stage, but now she can only watch.

"Sarah, it seems you're quite good at playing the piano. Do you remember how you started learning?" Fraser asks as he leads Sarah to the piano bench." Did you learn from a teacher or teach yourself through YouTube?"

"I have a piano teacher. She's been teaching me for seven years," Sarah responds as she sits down. "What would you like me to play?"

Fraser doesn't answer immediately. "Most of my friends know I don't play piano," he says, glancing at Kelsi and smiling. "I'm a bad student and struggle to learn, no matter how good the teacher is. But I've discovered that I can actually play piano quickly."

He reaches into his backpack and pulls out a biking helmet attached to a pair of goggles. "I've discovered I can replicate finger movements just by watching someone play once—I'm a visual learner. So, pick your favorite piece, about three to four minutes long, play it, and see if I can repeat it."

"But we thought this is a magic show!" someone in the audience calls out. "And you're playing the piano?"

"In the eyes of the Lord, none of us can perform magic but Him!" Fraser deftly evades the question. "For a guy who doesn't play piano, sitting down and playing a song is already magical, especially after hearing it only once." He puts on the helmet with goggles." This helps me to focus... *'and I will be still and know You're God'...*" he hums and steps to the left side of the piano, watching Sarah's slender fingers rest on the keys. He takes a deep breath and says, "You may start now."

Sarah begins playing "Theme from Love Story." Fraser watches closely, his head barely moving. Meanwhile, Kelsi thinks, *why is she picking this song? This is our song! I've played this with him at least three times!* She recalls Sarah's smile at him.

Sarah plays very well, close to Henry Mancini's version, but she hits a couple of wrong keys, perhaps intentionally. When she finishes, the audience claps loudly. She stands up, faces the audience, takes a bow, and steps down.

Fraser takes her place at the bench. "Now it's my turn. Dear Lord, we all know only You can perform miracles, but please give me strength and power to complete this act, in Your honor." For Fraser, every experiment is also a prayer — a bridge between the mind's logic and the heart's faith.

He rests his hands on the keys, stays still for a few seconds, and starts playing.

The audience thinks they're hearing a recording of Sarah's performance from earlier, even catching the same few wrong notes Sarah has slipped in on purpose during her performance. Kelsi can't believe her ears. *He tells me he doesn't play piano, and he can play like this? What else is he hiding from me?*

"... she fills my heart with very special things, with angel songs, and wild imagining..." Suddenly Kelsi hears him start singing softly, away from the microphone. Since she's sitting in the front row, the words are clear to her. It feels like he's singing just for her, and she's touched.

Suddenly the music stops, ending a bit earlier than when Sarah finished her piece.

The audience is silent for a moment before bursting into applause. *Is he singing to me?* Kelsi wonders, mesmerized. Then she hears his cell group brothers yelling, "Hey, keep singing... Kelsi, walks onto the stage..." They've all seen Fraser and Kelsi together often enough to immediately know who he's singing to. Fraser rarely sings, and when he does, it must mean something.

Fraser stands up, turns around, and takes off his helmet. "Oh Lord, thanks for letting me finish this piece... and please, let the brothers down there shut up..." He laughs, looking at Sarah. "Thanks, Sarah, for giving me an easy piece. To be honest, I've heard this song several times, but I've never played it. Honor to our Lord!"

He looks up, raising his right hand. "There's another person I should thank for playing this song to me before... Kelsi, come up here. You're also going to help me with my next act." He turns around and extends his hand to Kelsi, looking at her softly.

Heat rises to Kelsi's cheeks as the congregation calls her name. But when Fraser reaches out his hand, she stands up without a second thought and joins him. She has no idea what Fraser will say next, but she feels warm and excited. At the same time, two guys come from the back of the stage, each carrying an easel with charcoal pencils and paper. Fraser asks them to place one easel facing backstage and the other fifteen feet away, perpendicular to the first.

"For those of you who believe I know how to play piano and pretend I don't, you will be convinced of my visual learning ability by my next performance." Fraser gently grabs Kelsi's hand and leads her to stand in front of the first easel.

"Kelsi, besides playing the piano, I know you're a talented artist too. So please draw whatever you like on this canvas, and I'll try to draw the same on the other canvas. By standing there," he points to the spot in front of the second easel," I can only see your hands moving, but I can't see your canvas, at least not clearly. Now think of something you'd like to draw." As he puts on his helmet, he says softly, "You know how I love to see you draw..."

While the audience laughs, he steps in front of the second easel and picks up the charcoal pencil. "I'm ready when you are."

Kelsi closes her eyes for a few seconds, then picks up her pencil.

Nobody knows what Fraser is looking at through his goggles — Kelsi's lovely face or her delicate hands. But it's fascinating to see both of their hands moving in unison, fifteen feet apart. Kelsi is facing the audience, so no one can see what she is drawing. The easels are placed at the far back of the stage, making it impossible to see what Fraser is drawing either. After five minutes, Kelsi puts down her pencil and stands up. At the same time, Fraser also puts down his pencil, takes off his helmet, and stares at what he has just drawn. He doesn't say a word but looks bewildered.

Two guys come out from backstage. One takes Kelsi's easel, turns it around, and places it at the front of the stage for everyone to see. It shows a caricature of a young man's face, with exaggerated thick eyebrows and a large mouth with an unshaved chin. Everyone can recognize that she's drawing Fraser, and some start laughing and cheering.

As Kelsi looks at Fraser anxiously, the other guy takes Fraser's easel, turns it to face the audience, and puts it down. She sees a caricature of a young girl's face, with exaggerated large round eyes, a dimple on the chin, and thin, smiling lips. It's a picture of her.

Being a girl in love, she feels very sweet but somewhat confused. *"Why is he drawing a picture of me when he says he's replicating my drawing? I know he's not a good artist, but he draws so well..."*

Before she finishes her thoughts, a church brother stands up. "Fraser, you've just shown us two hidden talents we never knew about, but this isn't magic. We know you two will become one eventually, but today you are supposed to draw yourself, not her!"

Another church brother stands up. "Hey Fraser, do you have an announcement to make?" Everybody bursts into laughter.

8

Fraser stands up slowly, looks up, and says quietly, "Lord, I don't know why I can't trace Kelsi's hands, but there must be a reason. Thank You for letting me finish today's program." He walks toward Kelsi, holds her hand, and turns around to face the audience.

"I'm sorry our telepathy doesn't work this time, Andy," he says jokingly to the first brother. " I should have known what she is drawing. I always do." He chuckles. "Maybe I didn't expect her to draw me in front of everybody? Gosh, thank you Lord for giving me such a wonderful Christmas present!"

He takes Kelsi's other hand, holds them both in his palms, and kisses her on her cheek. Everybody starts laughing and clapping. Kelsi can only look at him softly and smile.

Sarah forces a smile, clapping along with everyone else. She tells herself she's happy for them — and she is — but a sharp little ache surprises her, catching her off guard. *Why does it bother me that he looks at Kelsi that way?* She bows her head quickly, whispering a prayer for grace, ashamed of the thought.

Fraser then speaks to the second brother. "Yes, Michael, I do have an announcement to make... No, it's not what you think... We will meet for our next fellowship this coming Sunday, and I'll bring my signature mochi cakes to share!"

Everybody laughs as Fraser and Kelsi walk off the stage.

Sarah, standing next to the stage, notices that Fraser has left his backpack. She immediately picks it up and rushes to Fraser and Kelsi.

"Fraser, you left your backpack!"

"Oh, thanks!" Fraser takes the backpack and puts it on his back.

Sarah then turns to Kelsi. "You draw very well! So lively and you captured his features perfectly!" she says.

"Why, thank you! You play piano very well too! You're Sarah, right? I'm Kelsi." The girls shake hands and smile at each other.

Chapter 2 *Songs and Secrets*

Confession of Love and Risk

Back in Fraser's apartment, the smell of freshly brewed coffee fills the air. Fraser and Kelsi sit across from each other, with the backpack on the coffee table. They stare at each other for a moment and start laughing.

"Fritz, you owe me an explanation," Kelsi says, using her affectionate nickname for Fraser when they are alone. "What exactly is this visual learning thing you talked about today? And can you really play piano and draw? Why have you been hiding your talents from me? I dream that one day we can perform together in your church choir."

"No, Kelsi, I can't play or draw. Scout's honor," Fraser replies, slowly pulling out his helmet and goggles. "You know I'm doing research in Artificial Intelligence. Right now, we're training machines to do a lot of things, but they're still just machines. What if a machine could train a human to go beyond their natural capabilities?" He speaks with the intensity of someone who doesn't just dream of progress, but of miracles hidden in code.

He looks Kelsi in the eyes and continues, "What if AI could translate what you see into instructions you could follow to replicate it?"

"So this is what trains you to learn piano and drawing?" Kelsi quickly grasps the concept, pointing to the helmet and goggles. "I've never heard of this before."

"This is what I've been researching at Berkeley. I'm working with Dr. Johnson and Dr. Stephens at Stanford on digitizing brainwaves and understanding how they interact with the physical body," Fraser explains, showing her the wires connecting to the goggles.

"The goggles' lenses capture and digitize my vision, transmitting data via Bluetooth to the computer in my backpack. After analyzing, the AI host sends instructions to my helmet, which communicates with my brain and tells me how to act."

"Wow, you can program these pieces to do all that? How smart can you get?" Kelsi says, amazed. She has always known Fraser is good with computer technology, but she never imagines he is a genius at this level. To her, he's just a kind and witty engineer who always cheers her up and makes her laugh. He's nothing like the stereotype nerd who talks about computers and AI all day.

She thinks for a few seconds, then says, "It seems like it didn't work out exactly as you intended, did it?"

She picks up her coffee cup and takes a sip. "You started singing before you finished Sarah's piece, and you drew me instead of yourself. Was that intentional?"

She hopes he'll say yes. Having a genius like him sing her song and draw her portrait would fill her heart.

"I think I miscalculated something, Kelsi," Fraser admits, pulling his chair closer to hers. "I programmed the human mind like a machine, which can learn and replicate instructions. But humans have emotions and feelings that can't be accounted for."

He moves closer and gently holds her hand. "When I got to the third verse, I suddenly remembered the time you played this song in the dorm lounge, and we sang together. I thought about you and couldn't help but sing... so I had to stop."

"Oh, that's so sweet. Were you embarrassed?" Kelsi whispers, leaning her head on Fraser's shoulder.

"Yes, a little," Fraser replies, putting his arm around her. "But I've been wanting to sing that to you for a while."

"Aww... Then why didn't your AI instructor tell you to follow my hands to draw yourself? When I saw my picture, I felt so... so touched. I know you're not a good artist." Kelsi closes her eyes for a moment, thinking about the moment she saw her portrait.

"I can't figure that out either," Fraser says, holding her tighter. "When I was looking at your hands, I couldn't actually see what I was drawing. Maybe when I started the program, I couldn't help but look at your face before moving to your hands. As I said, I haven't accounted for human feelings and emotions. So my AI algorithm instructs me to draw your face."

He gazes into her eyes. "The face I want to see every day..."

He starts to lose a little control. "I love you, Kelsi," he lifts her chin gently, his eyes meeting hers before their lips touch.

Kelsi feels a warm current flowing through her body, her heart pounding. She never has imagined this moment would occur. She wraps her arms around his neck and whispers, "Fritz, I love you too."

In that moment, research and reason fall away; only love remains, uncalculated and unstoppable.

As they savor the moment, Fraser's phone rings. He reluctantly picks it up.

"Hello, Fraser. Merry Christmas!" Jalen says.

"You call just to say Merry Christmas? Do you know you're interrupting a very important project, my friend?" Fraser pretends to be annoyed. But Jalen is his high school and college buddy. They can talk about anything and never get mad at each other.

"Hey, it's Christmas. You wouldn't be working on important projects during the holidays. I've known you for over ten years. You must be with Kelsi now, right?"

"Well, is that an important project? And how do you know I'm with her?" Fraser is a little grouchy.

"I tried calling her, but I got a DO NOT DISTURB message. Is that clear enough?" A girl's voice chimes in. It's Sabrina, Jalen's fiancée.

Kelsi quickly grabs Fraser's phone. "Sabrina, my phone battery died, and I am charging it... I accidentally put it on DO NOT DISTURB mode..."

"You are with Fraser, aren't you?" Sabrina giggles. "Say no more. Let's have Christmas dinner together tomorrow night. I'll make a reservation."

— ✦ —

Sabrina and Kelsi have been best friends since seventh grade. Sabrina also knows Fraser well because he frequently plays tennis with Jalen, and the three of them often hang out together. She sees Fraser as very smart and good-natured, but his busy schedule leaves him little time to meet new friends. Then she thinks of her friend Kelsi, a shy girl who has just moved to Berkeley and probably hasn't made any new friends yet.

"Why not set them up on a date?" she suggests to Jalen. They don't know Fraser and Kelsi are already dating.

15

So, one night, Jalen takes Fraser to a high-class restaurant. As they sit down and chat, Fraser is unaware of what is happening until fifteen minutes later when Sabrina and Kelsi walk in. Before Sabrina and Jalen could say anything, Fraser and Kelsi look at each other and simultaneously exclaim, "Why are you here?" and start laughing.

"I just had lunch with you and now I'm stuck with you again?" Kelsi giggles.

"Guess this is God's plan through my best friends—we just have to go with it!" Fraser always comes up with a witty answer. "Thank You, Lord. I prayed to see her again after lunch, and You answer my prayer immediately." Fraser winks at Sabrina and Jalen.

"So, you knew each other?" It is Sabrina and Jalen's turn to speak simultaneously. They know they don't have to worry anymore.

The four of them have a fantastic time that night. It is at this very same restaurant that they are going to have Christmas dinner.

Kelsi throws the phone onto the couch. Fraser immediately wraps his hands around her waist. "Let's pick up where we left off," he whispers in her ear.

Suddenly, Kelsi has a thought. "Have you shared your research results with anyone? This is a significant invention, and you need to keep it confidential until you've decided what to do

16

with it," she says nervously. "I worry that while the church folks will see it as just a performance and not taking it seriously, other techies could recognize its value. You must find a way to protect your invention!" For Kelsi, love means not only sharing dreams but protecting them — guarding his brilliance from a world too quick to exploit it.

"No, you're the only one I've shared this with," Fraser says, letting go of her. "Of course, Dr. Johnson and Dr. Stephens know because they're part of my team. I used this evening's performance to test what I've programmed. I haven't even told Jalen and Sabrina." He thinks for a moment. "But you're right. I should discuss this concern with them and see what we should do."

"Can I come along? I could put my business skills to use and might be able to help with some legal issues."

"Sure, my dear," he says, holding her tight.

Suddenly, the phone rings again. This time it's Kelsi's phone. She reluctantly picks it up.

"Hi Sweetheart, this is your mom. Merry Christmas! We're on a business trip to New York next week and would like to stop by the Bay Area to see you. Is that okay?"

"Oh, Mom, of course! I'd love to see you and Dad. Let me know what day you arrive. You'll have a chance to meet Fraser, too! See you then." Kelsi hangs up and turns to Fraser, evidently excited. "Hey Fritz, my mom and dad are coming to see me! They'd love to meet you!"

Without letting go of her, Fraser replies, "I'd love to meet them too, Kelsi. You haven't told me much about your family, so this is a great chance for me to get to know them. But please, don't tell them I'm a nerd."

"A gentle, kind, and lovely nerd," Kelsi says, pressing her lips to his.

The next day, they meet Jalen and Sabrina at their favorite restaurant.

"I heard you performed a magic show at your church event yesterday. How was it?" Jalen asks.

"Not too bad. You both should come next time; it's really fun," Fraser replies, glancing at Kelsi.

Sabrina immediately notices the glow in Kelsi's eyes. "Tell us all about it," she giggles and gently shakes Kelsi's shoulder.

"Well, he performed two acts that didn't end very well..." Kelsi begins shyly, but a voice behind her interrupts.

"No, they ended well. He sang you a song and painted you a portrait!"

"Hey Andy, get out of here!" Fraser exclaims. It is Fraser's church brother, Andy, walking by and teasing him.

"We didn't know you sang and drew so well. You could be a street artist in Berkeley after you get your degree if no jobs come through," Andy laughs as he walks off.

"You drew her a portrait? Can we see it? I've never seen you draw anything!" Jalen exclaims in surprise. "And that is part of a magic show?"

Fraser is about to explain his visual learning research when Kelsi cuts in, "The church folks all knew he couldn't draw, so he surprised them with a portrait he had taken time to prepare earlier. It is a classic magic illusion." She skillfully prevents Fraser from revealing his AI research to Jalen and Sabrina.

Before Sabrina can ask any more questions, the waiter brings in the appetizers.

"Let's toast to Christmas and our friendship," Fraser says, raising his glass.

"And especially to our Kelsi and Fraser!" Sabrina adds as they look and smile at each other.

Chapter 3 *Two Encounters*

Comfortable and Uncomfortable

As Fraser drives her home, Kelsi asks him to pull over. "I feel a little dizzy. Can we rest for a minute?"

"Yes, madame," Fraser steers his SUV into a parking spot at the marina, offering a clear view of the bay. "Are you okay?" he asks, putting his arm around her shoulder.

"Oh, maybe I drank a little too much." Kelsi leans her head on Fraser's shoulder and closes her eyes. "I'll be fine."

As Fraser gently runs his hand through Kelsi's hair, enjoying the scent of her perfume, a car pulls in and parks ten feet from his SUV.

"Hey, Fraser, is that you?" a girl shouts from the sedan.

Fraser turns around, rolls down the window, and sees Sarah sitting in the passenger seat next to a guy. She looks so stunning in her evening gown that he almost doesn't recognize her. For a heartbeat, beauty and trouble arrive in the same dress. She opens the car door, walks over, and notices Kelsi sleeping on Fraser's shoulder.

"Oh, it really is you and Kelsi! Just came out from a party?" she says softly to avoid waking Kelsi. "Jordan, come over and meet our church leader, Fraser! "

She waves to her driver.

A young man in a tuxedo walks over, extends his hand, and says, "Nice to meet you, Fraser. I'm Jordan. It's getting late, and this isn't the safest place. I should take Sarah home." He gives a quick nod. "Take care." Then he takes Sarah's hand and leads her back to the car.

As they walk away, Kelsi opens her eyes. "Seems like you have a contagious disease!" she whispers, giggling. "They walk away so quickly! " But beneath the joke, a thread of jealousy tugs at her heart.

"There are still at least ten cars around. It's not that unsafe," Fraser murmurs. " Why is this Jordan guy so hostile? Do I have bad breath?"

"My silly Fritz, if my gorgeous girlfriend can spot you from this distance at night and come over to greet you right away, I feel threatened!" Kelsi says, giggling.

Fraser feels a little stunned.

"No, you don't have bad breath," Kelsi says, wrapping her arms around his neck. "Let me prove it to you..." She presses her lips against his.

— ✦ —

In Jordan's car, Sarah is complaining. "Why didn't you let me talk to Fraser?"

"Couldn't you see the girl leaning on him? What would she think if she saw a pretty girl approaching and talking to her boyfriend?" Jordan explains.

"Oh, that's Kelsi. I know her too. She knows I'm just a friend..."

"Trust me, my girl, it doesn't work that way. Oh, isn't Fraser the one who played the piano and drew portrait at church yesterday?" Jordan suddenly remembers.

"Yes, he mentioned having this visual learning ability where he can replicate playing a tune just by watching me play it once. He says he can also draw whatever Kelsi draws by observing her hand movements, " Sarah says, clearly excited about Fraser's performance from yesterday.

"That's very interesting! Tell me more tomorrow when we meet for lunch," Jordan replies as he pulls over to the curb. He opens the car door and walks Sarah to her door. "See you tomorrow. Good night."

Jordan is a senior marketing manager at Alpha Venture Capital, and has a keen interest in AI applications. On his drive home, he recalls reading a report in a computer journal about digitizing human brainwaves through AI simulation. The study, co-authors by Dr. Johnson, Dr. Stephens, and Fraser Lin, fascinated him.

"Fraser? Is that Fraser Lin? " he wonders aloud, deciding to find out more information from Sarah.

— ✦ —

The phone rings just as Fraser is deep in thought, tinkering with a new idea — integrating a heuristic algorithm into the data input to simulate human feelings and emotions. He picks up the phone without looking away from his screen.

"Good morning, Fritz. My parents just got into San Francisco. They'll be staying at the Claremont Hotel for two days before heading to New York."

"Oh, when can I meet them?" Fraser asks, fingers still tapping the keyboard. "Dinner tonight, maybe?"

Sensing he's preoccupied, Kelsi lowers her voice. "I know you're swamped. I'll go pick them up. Let's meet at Chez Panisse at six. Love you." She hangs up.

Chez Panisse? That's unexpected, Fraser wonders. *Why did she choose this expensive restaurant?* Then he glances at the tall stack of ungraded reports beside him and sighs. Programming is easy. Grading all these papers before the semester starts? Not so much.

Feeling the need to clear his head, he grabs his keys and heads to the church gym for a round of basketball.

Before starting any activity, Fraser always visits the prayer room to pray. As he steps inside, he sees Sarah.

"Hey, Sarah, good morning. Do you come to pray often?" he asks with a smile.

"Good morning, Fraser, " Sarah replies with a lovely smile. "I need to make a presentation at school before the semester starts, so I'm praying for guidance and strength. By the way, I'm sorry for disturbing you and Kelsi at the marina last night. We have just come out from a party, and I am a little high. I hope Kelsi doesn't mind."

"Oh, it's alright. Kelsi had a bit too much to drink too, so we are just resting." Fraser starts walking out with Sarah, forgetting his prayer. "You mentioned a presentation at school? What do you do? "

"I teach seventh and eighth grade at a middle school, so we all have to prepare plans for the students before school starts," Sarah explains. "By the way, Fraser, it is so thoughtful of you to show your love to Kelsi that night! She must have been very touched. You two are such a good match! She's so beautiful and charming. Treasure her!" Sarah adds as she walks out of the church.

Her blessing is so genuine — but somehow, that truth hurts.

Fraser heads to the gym. It's empty. He picks up a basketball and starts shooting. Normally, he's a 30-percent shooter, but this time he misses 95 percent of the shots. He just can't concentrate - his hands know the form; his mind keeps slipping to a smile in an evening gown.

— ✦ —

Meanwhile, Jordan is waiting for Sarah in a Vietnamese restaurant, still pondering over what she says about Fraser's visual learning ability. *Is it what the report suggests? What an impact this research could have on the AI world! But is it really possible to replicate motions just by watching?* he wonders.

As he's lost in thought, Sarah walks in. "Have you been waiting long? " she asks, pulling out her chair and sitting down.

"No, only a few minutes," Jordan replies, handing her the menu.

"I'll have a medium pho tai and a hot Vietnamese coffee, please," she says to the waiter.

As they eat, Jordan asks, "I wasn't there to see when you explained Fraser's visual learning performance. How did it actually go?"

"Well, it starts as a magic show." Sarah begins. "Fraser pretended he couldn't play the piano or draw portraits, but then he surprised everyone by singing, playing the piano for his girlfriend, and even drawing her portrait in front of everyone to show his love. It is so romantic!" Sarah smiles and looks deeply at Jordan.

"Oh, he made it look so real. He even wore a helmet with goggles to show what he is using for this visual learning," she adds. " But everybody knew he is faking. I felt so happy for Kelsi! "

"What does Fraser do besides serving the church? I'd like to know him better, " Jordan says. "Maybe you can introduce me to him sometime? "

"I don't know him very well, but I heard he's a computer science research assistant at Berkeley. You two would have a lot to talk about." Sarah nods.

It is five-thirty. Fraser steps out of the shower, dresses semi-formally, and heads to Chez Panisse. Though it's only a fifteen-minute drive, his mind is preoccupied.

Initially, he thinks about his upcoming meeting with Dr. Johnson and Dr. Stephens. Then, his thoughts turn to meeting Kelsi's parents, which makes him quite nervous. Speaking confidently in front of hundreds in an auditorium is easy for him, but facing his girlfriend's parents is another story.

Suddenly, Sarah's image slips into his mind. He recalls what Kelsi said about her last night at the marina, and her friendly smile he saw this morning. He shakes his head several times. "This is not right," he mutters to himself.

He enters the restaurant, confirms the reservation, and takes a seat. He tries to focus on his human interaction programming and nothing else. Ten minutes later, Kelsi walks in with an elderly couple.

"Hey, Fritz, you're here already? " Kelsi spots him instantly and waves. "Come meet my parents! "

Fraser immediately stands up, walks over, and gives Kelsi a quick peck on the lips. Then he turns to the couple. "Hi, you must be Mr. and Mrs. Jiang. I'm Fraser. Very nice to meet you both. "

"Oh, Fraser, Kelsi talked so much about you, " Kelsi's mom replies with a smile as they all head to the table.

Fraser goes around and pulls out their chairs before sitting down himself.

"Welcome to the Bay Area, Mr. and Mrs. Jiang! " Fraser begins. "Is this your first time in California? "

"Oh, I visit the States twice a year, mostly the East Coast, for business, " Mr. Jiang replies, eyeing Fraser. "My wife doesn't come as often. This is our second time in California. "

"Most of the time, I stay in Hong Kong to manage our business there, " Mrs. Jiang adds. "By the way, please call us Uncle and Auntie." She smiles warmly at Kelsi.

The waiter brings in a bottle of champagne.

"Let's cheer up! " Mr. Jiang raises his glass.

As they enjoy their appetizers, Mr. Jiang turns to Fraser. "I heard you're a computer engineer at Berkeley. What exactly do you do? "

"I'm a research assistant pursuing my doctorate. I specialize in Artificial Intelligence applications," Fraser replies, glancing at Kelsi. He hesitates, unsure if he should disclose more about his work on visual learning technology.

Sensing his uncertainty, Kelsi quickly jumps in. "Mom, Dad, Fraser is very talented. Just a few days ago, he pretended to perform magic and used the opportunity to sing and paint a portrait for me! "

"Oh, really? You can sing and draw? You have to show me her portrait so we can frame it!" Mrs. Jiang exclaims cheerfully. "Kelsi draws very well too. You two have a lot in common!"

The waiter brings in the main entrée.

As they eat, Mrs. Jiang suddenly asks Fraser, "Do you like cooking?"

"Yes, I cook often, but I'm not very good," Fraser replies politely. " I'm still a student and so busy that I often don't have time to eat out." He refrains from mentioning that finances are tight in front of this family.

"Mom, he's a very good cook," Kelsi interjects. "He's made dinner for me a couple of times, and his steamed fish is top-notch! The meat is perfectly cooked, better than most restaurants!" She beams with pride.

"Well, you can't be a chef for life!" Mr. Jiang adds cheerfully. "Now, tell me what you plan to do after you get your degree." He looks at Fraser expectantly.

"I'm not sure, sir. I'll be getting my degree in two years. The economy is uncertain, and technological breakthroughs keep happening. I really don't have a plan right now," Fraser says, taking the opportunity to express his frustrations.

"Hey, son, if you can't find anything you like after graduation, you're welcome to work for me," Mr. Jiang says warmly. "We have software development teams in New York, Chicago, and Toronto. Think about it."

After dinner, Kelsi takes her parents back to their hotel and then meets Fraser for a drink.

"What did you think about my parents, Fritz? My dad calls you son! Seems they like you a lot," Kelsi asks.

"Oh, they are very kind and warm. I like them, " Fraser replies. "But you've never told me much about your family background. What do your dad and mom do? "

"They run several types of businesses. Honestly, I'm not entirely sure what all they do," Kelsi says, holding Fraser's hand. "My dad travels a lot—to China, the States, and sometimes Europe. I don't see him very often. I spend much more time with my mom. She stays in Hong Kong to manage two restaurants." She squeezes Fraser's hand tightly, as if afraid he might slip away.

Fraser is silent for a moment. "I never thought you came from such a wealthy family," he says, suddenly pulling her into his arms. "But you're so congenial and approachable... why? I come from a poor family... how did I end up meeting you?"

The usually eloquent Fraser sounds like a man struggling to find the right words.

Kelsi holds him tighter. "I've never met anyone as genuine as you, Fritz," she whispers. "You're the most caring person in my life besides my family."

Tears begin to roll down her cheeks. Fraser gently lifts her chin, kisses away her tears, and presses his lips against hers.

Chapter 4   *Worlds Apart*

Can Love Conquer?

ও ও ও

Inside Limewood Restaurant at the Claremont Hotel, Mr. and Mrs. Jiang are having breakfast with Kelsi.

"How do you like Fraser?" Kelsi asks, anxiously awaiting their response.

"He's a nice young man." Mrs. Jiang's eyes twinkle. "I like anyone who can cook. "

"He is very intelligent and thoughtful, very different from the other guys you knew," Mr. Jiang adds. "I like him a lot." He is comparing Fraser with Kelsi's other boyfriends in Hong Kong. "Now tell me a little more about the church party and what he did that night."

As Kelsi describes Fraser's performance, Mr. Jiang comments, "He is holding a helmet with goggles to observe? That must mean something." He laughs and continues. "Computer engineers normally have a one-track mind and aren't very creative or romantic. He might be telling the truth about the visual learning process." As a successful businessman, Mr. Jiang is very keen with his observations.

Hearing this, Kelsi debates whether she should tell her parents about Fraser's research or remain silent. She knows her dad is very perceptive and quick to seize opportunities.

Then her dad asks, "Can we meet him again one more time in the morning? I'd like to see his helmet and goggles. We can have lunch together before we board our plane."

Kelsi feels compelled to agree.

— ✦ —

Back inside Tri-City Church, Fraser is in the prayer room praying.

That morning, Fraser is supposed to meet up with Dr. Johnson and Dr. Stephens, but Dr. Stephens has to give a presentation at UCLA and is unavailable. Fraser is actually relieved that the meeting is postponed because his mind is cluttered with thoughts and he cannot think straight.

Why is Kelsi from such a wealthy family? What happened last night runs through his mind. *We love each other so much, but can this work out when our backgrounds are worlds apart? I really couldn't afford Chez Panisse, and yesterday's dinner cost me half a month's stipend already. I've been taking her out to McDonald's and getting Ranch 99 takeout, and she hasn't even said a word.*

But she's so casual with me when we're together. She doesn't act anything like a billionaire's daughter at all... He continues his thoughts, looking at the cross on the wall. *"Lord, in Your honor, please show me what to do. I'm weak, but You are strong. Please guide me to do the right thing,"* he prays.

As he steps out, he sees Sarah walking in.

"Hi, Sarah," he glances at her, nods, and keeps walking.

Sarah stops him. "Hey Fraser, you look worried. Is something bothering you?" she asks.

"Oh, nothing serious. I'm just thinking about my research report." He turns around, gives Sarah a smile, and continues on his way out. For some reason he can't quite understand, he doesn't want to chat with Sarah alone. But Sarah won't let him go.

"Fraser, you say your cell group is meeting this coming Sunday. Can my boyfriend and I join you?" she asks politely. "He's Jordan, the person you met the other night at the marina."

The word boyfriend rings like a bell he doesn't expect to hear. But he still says, "Sure, anybody is welcome to join. Can I have your phone number so I can send you more details about our meeting?" He can't believe he's asking Sarah for her contact number.

Once Fraser gets back to his office, he picks up his students' reports and starts grading them, trying to focus on something other than Kelsi and Sarah. Just then, Kelsi calls.

"Hey Fritz, my parents would like to meet you for lunch tomorrow before they leave for New York," she says warmly. "Bring your helmet and goggles too. Dad wants to see them. I think we can let him know what you're up to. He should have the resources to make our plan happen!"

"Sure, Kelsi. I'll come to Claremont at ten. I have so much to do today. See you tomorrow." He hangs up quickly, unsure why he feels so rushed.

— ✦ —

Later that day, Sabrina calls.

"Hey Fraser, I heard you finally met Kelsi's parents. How did it go?" she asks curiously. "Kelsi had a few boyfriends in Hong Kong, but her parents didn't like any of them. Now it's your turn!"

"Sabrina, you never told me she came from such a wealthy family! I am stunned and don't know what to do," Fraser complains. "Her boyfriends must have been quite rich too..."

"Her father and Jalen's father are business partners and competitors," Sabrina replies. "We are supposed to introduce her to you, but it turns out you already knew each other very well. So we assumed you know her background."

"She told me that her parents like you, Fraser. You are very talented, especially in cooking. We should know..." Sensing his concern, Sabrina starts teasing him to help him relax. "Jalen and I can tell she likes you a lot, more than anyone we've seen before. I know her very well. True love always trumps money!"

He wants to believe her; at that time, he does.

He feels much better after Sabrina hangs up. He then sets up a conference call with Dr. Johnson and Dr. Stephens to discuss some technical issues he encounters during his trial at the church event. During the conversation, he brings up the subject of human feelings and emotions. They all agree that the prototype is not yet ready for prime time and requires further research.

It's four P. M., too early for dinner and too late to start anything new. Normally, Fraser would meet up with Kelsi at this time, but since she's with her parents and they'll see each other the next day anyway, he decides to go for a drive to clear his mind.

As he drives, he passes a middle school and sees Sarah in the playground, playing with two kids. One girl is in a wheelchair, and the other boy is holding a cane, apparently struggling to see well. School has not started yet, so he is surprised to see Sarah at the school with her students.

"Hi, Sarah, I didn't expect to see you at school at this time," Fraser says as he steps out of the car and greets her.

"Hi, Fraser. These are my neighbor's kids. She went to buy groceries and asked me to babysit for a couple of hours, " Sarah explains, with her usual lovely smile on her face.

Fraser isn't used to dealing with physically challenged kids. Noticing his expression, Sarah adds, "They are siblings." She points to the girl. "Katie has cerebral palsy. She can't walk and has very limited use of her hands. "

Pointing to the boy, she continues, "Charlie was very sick at the age of two and had lost over 95 percent of his eyesight. Their mom Maria is divorced and has to take care of them alone. The alimony barely covers living expenses, let alone medical bills." She sighs. "I live only a block away, so I often babysit for her so she can have some time to herself. Normally I walk them to my school playground to play."

"It's so kind of you to help this family, Sarah," Fraser says, looking deeply into her eyes. "Can I take you out to dinner after their mother returns? Kelsi is with her parents, and I don't like eating alone. I'll wait with you." He can't believe he's asking her out.

Sarah is a little surprised but seems delighted. "Let me call home first."

As she is making the call, a woman walks onto the playground. "Thanks so much, Sarah," she says, placing one hand on the wheelchair and grabbing Charlie's cane with the other before leaving with the kids.

"No problem, Maria!" Sarah says, waving to the kids. "My mom says it's okay, but I have to be home before seven." She then turns to Fraser. "We can't go too far."

Fraser opens the passenger side door, allowing Sarah to get in. "I see there's a Vietnamese restaurant three blocks away that looks pretty decent. Do you like Vietnamese food?" he asks as he starts the engine.

"Oh, Pho 99? We go there occasionally. The food is pretty good, but my mom's cooking is better."

The restaurant isn't very crowded. Fraser orders a bowl of Bun Bo Hue, while Sarah chooses Pho Tai with meatballs. They have a great time chatting and laughing. For a moment he forgets everything else — until a small pang of conscience reminds him he shouldn't.

After driving Sarah home, Fraser goes to a Starbucks and sits down to ponder.

"The food at Chez Panisse is much better than at Pho 99, so why did I enjoy tonight's dinner more?" he wonders. *"Is it because of Sarah? No, that can't be it. I love eating with Kelsi too. Maybe it's because of Kelsi's parents?"* He tries to convince himself with various reasons, but the question fills him with guilt.

But the more he tries to push Sarah out of his mind, the more vividly he thinks about her. He reflects on poor Katie and Charlie, their struggling mother, and Sarah's kindness in helping them.

"Would Kelsi show the same compassion?" The thought strikes him suddenly. It's hard to imagine a billionaire's daughter taking the time to help a family like this.

He doesn't want to dwell on his thoughts any longer, so he heads to the church. It's past nine O'clock, and the building is empty and still. He walks into the prayer room. This time

37

Sarah is not there. He kneels and gazes at the golden cross on the wall.

"Lord, thank You for giving me Kelsi. But why do You bring Sarah into my life?" he prays, tears in his eyes. He doesn't want another door; he barely knows how to guard the one he has. *"They are both angels to me. Please help me understand why You bring them into my life and show me how they are shaping my journey according to Your will."*

Before he can say Amen, he sees the cross shimmering in the moonlight streaming through the window, as if God is speaking to him. Instantly, a sense of calm washes over him.

He walks out, gets into his SUV, and closes his eyes. The image of Maria pushing the wheelchair with one hand and guiding Charlie with the other, flashes in his mind. *My Lord, I pray that You will help this family,* he whispers before starting the engine.

As he drives, he turns on the radio to listen to some music.

"… I say, God, why don't You do something? He says, I do, I created you! "

It's Matthew West's "Do Something", a song Fraser has listened to many times before. But this time, it hits him like an arrow.

"I ask God, and He says He created me.. He gave me the intelligence to research the visual learning process... because He wants me to use it to help those in need... "

Suddenly, his mind clears. The images of Kelsi and Sarah fade away, replaced by the vision of a helmet with attached goggles.

— ✦ —

The next morning, Fraser wakes up early. He puts on his workout gear, jogs for half an hour, and takes a shower. Grabbing his backpack, he heads to the Claremont Hotel.

Inside Mr. and Mrs. Jiang's suite, Kelsi is chatting with her mom.

"Remember Peter? He just got engaged to Mr. Yang's daughter," her mom says with a light laugh. "After you broke up with him, he found someone else within three months."

"I never liked him. He is such a control freak," Kelsi chuckles.

Then the phone rings. "There's a Mr. Lin here to see you," the receptionist says.

"Let him in, and please bring some coffee and pastries too."

"Good morning, Uncle and Auntie," Fraser says as he steps in, giving Kelsi a quick peck on the lips.

"Please, sit down. Have you had breakfast yet? Here's some coffee and pastries." Mrs. Jiang pulls him over enthusiastically. "Kelsi mentioned that you make amazing banana bread and mochi cakes. How do yours compare to these pastries? " She can't help but stay on the topic of food.

"No, Auntie, I just bake for fun. Kelsi is easy to impress; I just add extra sugar." Fraser replies with his usual wit. Kelsi playfully punches his shoulder, and they all laugh together.

39

"It's not easy to find someone who's good at both cooking and baking," Mrs. Jiang praises Fraser.

"And a computer genius too!" Mr. Jiang adds cheerfully. "So, can you draw a portrait of Kelsi just by looking at her side profile? You're like another Da Vinci!" he jokes, blending humor with a clever remark.

Fraser feels the pressure mounting. He can't admit to switching the drawing in front of hundreds, as Kelsi tells Sabrina and Jalen. If he does, Mr. Jiang would surely ask how the trick is done, and he has no clue. Seeing Kelsi nodding slightly, he opens his backpack and pulls out his helmet and goggles.

"Uncle, that's what I use," Fraser explains, pointing to the goggles. "The goggles capture what I see and communicate with my computer in the backpack, which then sends instructions to my brain to follow." He summarizes the process neatly in one sentence.

Mr. Jiang fiddles with the helmet for a few seconds before saying, "This reminds me of something I read in a computer journal some time ago. We are exploring technological innovations when a friend showed me an article he co-authored."

He pulls out his iPad, quickly swipes, and shows Fraser a report. "I've known Thomas Johnson for years. Is this you?" He points to the name "Fraser Lin" in the report.

"Yes, Uncle, it's me." Fraser knows he can no longer hide his research. "This is a prototype I developed, but it still has many issues we need to tackle," he admits.

"This research has great potential. If you prefer, I can have my development team contact you for any support you need," Mr. Jiang offers.

He then turns to Kelsi and says, "He needs concentration and encouragement to do his work, and I leave that up to you, my girl." He pats Kelsi on the shoulder. "If you need anything, just let your mom and me know."

Chapter 5 *Dreams of Healing*

Sacred Vision vs. Earthly Plot

After watching her parents depart, Kelsi meets up with Fraser for dinner. "I missed you so much yesterday, Fritz," she says, hugging him tightly as if never wanting to let go. "Where are we going for dinner?" she asks.

"How about a Vietnamese restaurant?" Fraser suggests without thinking. He pretends it's about food; his heart knows better. He wants to see how Kelsi compares to Sarah while eating similar cuisine in a more modest setting.

"Oh, let's try that," she responds without hesitation.

Fraser chooses a restaurant near the campus, avoiding Pho 99 where he's afraid of running into Sarah. He can't quite explain why.

During their meal, Kelsi remarks, "It seems Dad is really interested in your research. He must have a good sense of what the visual learning program can achieve in practical applications. We should definitely ask for his opinion when he returns from his trip." Evidently, she is excited due to her parents' encouragement.

Fraser remains silent for a moment, then suddenly asks, "Kelsi, is your dad involved in any healthcare businesses?"

"I think he is sitting on the boards of two hospitals, why do you ask?" Kelsi wonders aloud.

"Because last night, I had a vision that I need to use my research to help those who can't see or control their bodies," Fraser explains emotionally. "God gave me this intelligence, and I feel I must put it to good use."

Kelsi is taken aback; she has never heard him speak this way before even though she knows he's a Christian. Coming from a wealthy family, she hasn't given much thought to the challenges faced by the less fortunate and disabled.

"But even if I can create devices to help, welfare and Medicare can't cover the expenses," Fraser continues, venting his frustrations. "I hate to say it, but your dad is a businessman." He sighs. "Producing these devices is expensive, and they may be out of reach for these folks because they can't afford them." He hates the math that measures mercy.

Kelsi reaches out to hold his hands. "I'm not sure that's what Dad has in mind, but where there's a will, there's a way," she whispers softly in his ear. "I'll always be by your side."

After dinner, Fraser drives Kelsi to the marina to watch the sunset. As they hold hands and gaze at the ocean, Fraser says, "Remember Sarah? I ran into her by chance yesterday, and we ended up having dinner together." Something inside him tells him he shouldn't hide anything from Kelsi. He chooses honesty. Love is clearer when nothing is hidden.

"Oh, I was with Mom and Dad all day yesterday, so I'm glad you found someone to have dinner with," Kelsi says naturally, without a hint of jealousy. She trusts Fraser completely. "How did you run into her?" she asks.

"I am driving aimlessly and saw her playing with two disabled kids in a schoolyard," Fraser replies, feeling a sense of relief. He then shares Maria's story with Kelsi. "I feel so sorry for Maria and her two kids," he sighs.

"Wasn't Jordan with Sarah? " Kelsi asks.

"No, it is just her," Fraser replies, not sure why Kelsi mentions this. He adds, "Maybe he is at work. I hope he won't mind if he finds out Sarah had dinner with me."

"Maybe he will, maybe he won't," Kelsi says with a giggle, wrapping her hand around Fraser's arm. "If he trusts Sarah like I trust you, it'll be fine." Then she leans in and whispers softly, "Love is patient, love is kind. It does not envy, it does not boast, it is not proud..."

Fraser is astonished and delighted to hear her recite 1 Corinthians 13. He can't help embracing her tightly and kissing her.

Before driving Kelsi back, Fraser suddenly says, "Let me show you where I go to pray when I'm feeling down. God always answers my prayers." He parks his SUV in front of the church and walks in, hand in hand with Kelsi.

As they enter the prayer room, they see Sarah praying, tears glistening in her eyes.

"Hey Sarah, it's quite late and you're still here? Is something bothering you? " Fraser asks, approaching her with concern.

"Hi Fraser, hi Kelsi," Sarah replies softly, her usual lovely smile not there. "I didn't expect to see both of you here at this hour. I'm facing a big problem and I need God's guidance. "

"Can you share it with us, Sarah? Maybe we can help," Kelsi says, stepping closer. For some reason, she feels she can do something.

"Charlie is hit by a hit-and-run driver this morning," Sarah says emotionally. "The estimated medical bill is twelve thousand dollars. My neighbor Maria doesn't have that kind of money. I tried to get an advance on my paycheck, but I could only get three thousand. With our savings of two thousand, we're still seven thousand short. The bill is due tomorrow. I feel like I'm at a dead end."

Kelsi gazes into Sarah's teary eyes. "These are the eyes of an angel!" Her own eyes begin to well up with tears as she pulls out her checkbook, moved by something she can't ignore.

Fraser watches the two girls in silence, struck by the moment. He knows that seven thousand dollars doesn't mean much for a billionaire's daughter, but he is deeply moved by how swiftly and willingly Kelsi responds without hesitation.

As Kelsi signs the check, Sarah feels a small ache she doesn't expect.

She's always sensed that Fraser cares for her — and in some corner of her heart, she feels the same.

But watching Kelsi's quiet grace, Sarah understands something clearly: this is a love she should never stand against.

Whatever spark she felt, she must let go — the way an angel would.

Kelsi hands the check to Sarah. Sarah holds the check up high, facing the cross, and whispers, " Thank You, Lord. I pray, and You sent Your angel so quickly… blessed be Your name." She then looks at the check and sees it's for fifteen thousand dollars, a bit more than what she needs.

Before Sarah can say anything, Kelsi hugs her and says, "You don't have to use your savings or your advance pay. You need that money for your family too. The extra is for Maria to use as an emergency fund to take care of the kids."

Sarah's eyes fill with tears as she accepts the check. For the first time, Fraser sees that wealth is not the enemy. In Kelsi's hands, it becomes God's provision — an angel's gift. And in that moment, he knows his heart belongs with her.

Kelsi then turns to Fraser and softly continues, "Normally he doesn't take me to church at this time, but he did tonight. I feel like I was sent here for a purpose. I 've just met an angel."

Fraser watches the angels smile at each other, and he now understands why God brings them into his life.

Fraser remains silent as he drives Kelsi back, feeling grateful but doesn't know what to say. After he parks his SUV in front of her dorm, Kelsi breaks the silence.

"I feel so small compared to Sarah," she says, tears beginning to roll down her cheeks. "She's like a real angel, giving so much of her time and money to help others in need. And I am here..."

Humility looks so beautiful on her; he won't let it become shame. Fraser gently lifts her chin, looking into her eyes. "No, Kelsi, you are an angel who helps other angels. God sent us here to serve a purpose. One angel cannot do it alone." He kisses away her tears with a tender and reassuring touch.

That next Sunday morning, about thirty people are gathering in the church's conference room. Fraser places a large box on the table and suggests, "Let's have something to eat before we begin our fellowship." He opens the box, revealing dozens of mini cupcakes. Kelsi busily distributes them to everyone.

"Hi Fraser! Hi Kelsi!" Sarah and Jordan greet as they walk in. Jordan notices a backpack in the corner, pulls up a chair, and sit next to it. Sarah picks up the cupcake in front of her, takes a bite, and exclaims, "This tastes so good! Are you sure you made these, not Kelsi? "

"He's the best baker around, only second to 85°C and Paris Baguette, "Fraser's church brother Andy jokes. "If not for his baking, half of us wouldn't be here!" Laughter erupts among the group.

"Before we begin, let's welcome Sarah and her friend Jordan. It's their first time joining us, so let's make them feel welcome," Fraser cheerfully announces to start the meeting.

After the meeting, when Fraser comes to pick up his backpack, Jordan asks, "Can we have lunch together today? You're a computer scientist, and I have something to consult you on. Do you mind?"

"Not at all. You pick a restaurant, Kelsi and I will join," Fraser replies, one hand holding Kelsi's and the other grabbing his backpack.

They decide on a Thai restaurant and order Angel Wings, Pad Thai, Tom Yum Goong, and Green Curry to share. Sarah sits next to Kelsi, chatting about their piano experiences and other girl talk.

Jordan sits next to Fraser. "When Sarah told me about your church performance, I am amazed," he says, glancing at Fraser's backpack. "She mentioned you are using a helmet and goggles to capture motion for replication. It's fascinating."

He then pulls out his iPad, swiping to a report. "This is just like what this report describes. Are you Fraser Lin? "

Fraser chuckles lightly. "There aren't many Frasers around. Yes, that's me. But it's really Dr. Johnson and Dr. Stephens who do most of the work; I just tag along."

"But your goggles do capture and digitize what you see and send the signals to your brain, right?" Jordan persists to seek more details. "Can I see your helmet and goggles?"

Fraser hesitates for reasons he can't quite explain. "I left them at home. They are just props for the show and don't really mean much," he says, trying to deflect further discussion.

The waiter brings all the entrées at once.

"Let's dig in!" Fraser exclaims, steering his conversation with Jordan away from further discussions about his report.

As they're about to finish, Fraser's phone starts to buzz. He picks it up.

"Hey, Dr. Stephens? You're back in the Bay Area now? Great, I'll meet you at Stanford at two." He sounds excited. Turning to the others, he exclaims, "Dr. Stephens has finally solved two major issues in my research! I will get results much faster than I expected! "

"I've already paid the waiter. We'll see you all later. Have a great day!"

With one hand holding Kelsi's and the other carrying the now empty cupcake box, he walks away, forgetting his backpack.

As Fraser is driving, Kelsi asks, "What do you think of Sarah and Jordan? They seem to be a good match." Perhaps she is testing him.

"Physically, they make a good pair. Jordan isn't a Christian, but if he's interested in joining a fellowship, he should go with Sarah's," Fraser shares his thoughts. "He didn't talk much, but he kept eyeing my backpack." Fraser chuckles. "He's clearly more interested in my research and my visual learning prototype than sharing the words of God."

"Backpack?" Kelsi turns to look at the passenger seat. "It's not here. You left it at the restaurant!" she yells anxiously. "Turn back!"

— ✦ —

At Alpha Venture Capital, Jalen is in his office reading reports. Even on a Sunday, AVC remains staffed to stay competitive in Silicon Valley. Jalen usually doesn't come in on weekends, but today he's preparing a presentation and getting ready for his trip back to Hong Kong. The company is owned by his father, Mr. Chang, and Jalen is serving as its Executive President.

His secretary calls, "Jordan from the marketing department would like to see you."

"Let him in," Jalen responds, aware that his committee has tasked the marketing team with researching state-of-the-art AI applications. Jordan, the senior marketing manager, enters the office carrying a backpack.

"Do you have your report ready?" Jalen asks.

"Going on a trip after this meeting?" Jalen adds with a casual tone, as he often does with his employees.

"No, sir," Jordan replies politely, presenting his iPad. "But I found something very interesting." He swipes to a report. "This study on visual learning through AI observations is fascinating. It's authored by a PhD student at Berkeley. Interestingly, the author, Fraser Lin, happens to be a friend of my girlfriend."

"Fraser? Visual learning?" Jalen recalls their conversation in the restaurant about Fraser's church performance. "But this is just a research paper. Do you see a practical application for it at this stage?" he questions Jordan.

"I believe the research has paid off. At a church event, Fraser Lin wore a helmet with goggles to demonstrate. He can replay the song my girlfriend plays on the piano just by watching her hands once," Jordan describes eagerly to his boss. He knows that if he can successfully sell his discovery, an instant promotion awaits him.

"Oh really? I'll have to see this helmet and goggles prototype to believe it," Jalen smiles, hinting that the meeting is over.

"But Mr. Chang, I actually have the prototype with me!" Jordan quickly points to the backpack. "This afternoon, I had lunch with Fraser Lin and he left his backpack at the restaurant."

He eagerly places his hands on it. "Since I don't have his phone or address, I can't return it to him right away. I thought you might be interested in seeing it first, so I brought it straight to you."

He unzips the backpack, and both he and Jalen peer intently inside.

Chapter 6 *The Forgotten Backpack*

Divine or Coincidence?

"Turn back! What if someone grabbed your backpack and helmet? Why are you still driving straight?" Kelsi pats Fraser's right arm urgently.

"We have to meet Dr. Stephens at Stanford in an hour. There's no time to turn back." Fraser replies calmly. "The helmet and goggles are of no use to anybody. Only I can use them, my dear," he adds with a mischievous smile. "Don't worry, Sarah and Jordan probably picked up the backpack for me. I'll ask Sarah tonight."

"What if someone as genius as you grabbed it? They could hack it and reverse-engineer it, ruining your chance to patent it," Kelsi frets with business concern.

"They won't," Fraser says, laughing. "Trust me, everything will be fine. God will provide."

Back in Jalen's office at AVC, Jordan opens the backpack. What he pulls out is a stack of bibles.

"You think putting this on your head will make you learn and repeat motions?" Jalen can't help laughing. "Maybe you can learn and replicate by praying?"

Jordan, shocked to find the helmet missing, stammers, "I don't know... he wasn't carrying his helmet and goggles today." Then he remembers this is exactly what Fraser told him during lunch.

"I'm really sorry, Mr. Chang. Let me find out more details about this research," Jordan says, slowly walking out with the backpack. His stomach twists. He tells himself he's just doing his job, but deep down he knows he has crossed a line he barely understands. He grips the strap harder and keeps walking.

Meanwhile, Jalen is deep in thought.

"I know Fraser very well. If he published this in a paper, he must have solid evidence," Jalen muses, weighing Fraser's personality." But a device so important to him would always be with him. He wouldn't leave it at home. Could it be just a prop for his show, as Kelsi suggested? He's funny and witty, but this doesn't seem like him. I have to talk with him to find out." Jalen admires Fraser's wit, though he notices that behind the jokes Fraser carries a quiet seriousness about his work.

Meanwhile, after the meeting with Dr. Stephens, Fraser and Kelsi are on their way back.

"Dr. Stephens finally gave me enough information about cerebral palsy. I can start working on the application tomorrow," Fraser tells Kelsi cheerfully. "Let's head back and enjoy the mochi cupcakes I made for you." Fraser always saves some of the pastries he bakes for church, adding a special twist to surprise Kelsi.

As soon as Kelsi steps into Fraser's room, she notices a helmet with goggles on the desk, connected to a desktop computer.

"So you didn't put the helmet in your backpack? That's why you're so calm?" Kelsi exclaims, gently punching Fraser. "Why didn't you tell me in the car?"

Fraser grabs her hand and pulls her into an embrace as he explains. "This morning, I was transferring data between the goggle host and the computer when I encountered a glitch. After fixing it, the data transfer became painfully slow, and I had to leave for church without them."

"Knowing Sarah and Jordan would be at my fellowship, I grabbed a couple of bibles for them just in case." He chuckles. "I think our Lord knew someone would take my backpack today and made sure I filled it with His words instead."

Kelsi cannot stop laughing until Fraser seals her lips with his own.

After a long while, Fraser finally calls Sarah while Kelsi is playing with his helmet.

55

"Hey Sarah, this afternoon I left my backpack in the restaurant. Did you or Jordan pick it up?" he asks.

"Glad you called, Fraser. We picked it up, but we weren't sure how to return it to you because I don't have your contact information. So I ask Jordan to keep it in his car until I can get your contact details from church tomorrow," Sarah speaks with relief.

"No problem, Sarah. By the way, how's Charlie doing after the surgery? He's so young," Fraser expresses his concern. "I'd love to meet him and assess his needs so I can start developing a prototype helmet and goggles for him."

"Oh, Charlie's doing remarkably well. He's about 90 percent recovered now. Really? You can make something to help him see? That's a miracle! Maria would be so... so happy!" Sarah pauses, her voice filled with emotion. "It's Katie that I'm really worried about. I wish there's something that could help her use her hands and legs. I feel so sad when she can't even feed herself."

Her voice falters. "Sometimes I don't understand why God lets Katie suffer this way. I pray every night, but when I see her struggle just to lift a spoon, I wonder if my prayers make any difference at all." The confession slips out before she can stop it, raw and unpolished. For a moment she feels guilty, as if doubting were a betrayal of her faith — yet she cannot deny the ache inside her heart.

She takes a deep breath and continues. "By the way, please thank Kelsi for me. She's truly an angel who appears just when we need help. I sincerely thank God for bringing such a beautiful angel into your life."

After Sarah hangs up, Kelsi stares at Fraser's phone. After a long pause, she finally says, "Sarah, you are an angel yourself."

— ✦ —

A few days later, Fraser and Kelsi visit Charlie's family. With school in session, Sarah can't be there with them. She has already shared Kelsi's kind action with Maria, who is forever grateful.

"Uncle Fraser, are you a friend of Auntie Sarah?" Charlie mutters. "Auntie Sarah is so nice to us." His speech is still halting.

"Yes, she really is. Charlie, can you see my hands?" Fraser starts by evaluating Charlie's vision.

"I cannot see. There are patches and shades. I don't know what they are," Charlie mutters repeatedly.

"That's okay. Now I'm sticking some strings to your hair and I'm putting a helmet on your head. Stay still..." Fraser explains patiently, connecting his laptop. He focuses intently on the screen, typing away, and occasionally glancing at Charlie to see how he's doing.

Kelsi is sitting next to Maria, watching Fraser's every move intently.

"I've never seen him this focused. He's always smiling and making me laugh when we're together," Kelsi says to Maria.

"When people are in love, they behave differently," Maria responds philosophically with a smile. "Sarah told me Mr. Fraser is very smart, and now I believe her. If he can really help Charlie, I don't know how to thank him..." She continues, her eyes glistening with tears. Maria isn't used to hope arriving in human form, yet here it is, bent over her son with quiet focus.

Kelsi admires Fraser with pride, yet a whisper of doubt creeps in — what if his world of science and miracles grows so vast that there's no place for her in it? She quickly pushes the thought aside, reminding herself that love isn't measured in equations but in presence, and she intends to stay by his side.

"I believe in him. He can do anything, if it's according to God's will," Kelsi chimes in. She can't believe she just says that, thinking she must have spent too much time with Fraser.

Then Fraser comes to a halt. He gently pats Charlie on the shoulder, looks at him warmly, and says," I got what I need. I think I can provide you with a new hat and a pair of glasses to help you very soon." Turning to Kelsi, he radiates a sense of accomplishment and satisfaction.

Kelsi meets his gaze. "Those are the eyes of an angel!" She feels a warm sense of gratification and pride. For a moment, she feels as though his gift is not his alone but something heaven itself has lent him.

That evening, Sarah is having dinner with Jordan.

"Hey Jordan, Fraser is for real. Today he came to Maria's house and worked on making a device to help Charlie see and walk better!" she says enthusiastically. "This can't be just for show. He must really know this kind of technology. So I think his visual learning performance is real too." She expresses her admiration for Fraser.

Jordan is silent for a moment. He hasn't mentioned to Sarah that he took the backpack to his boss to see, for obvious reasons. All he can say is, "Oh, that's great. I hope he succeeds in helping Charlie."

"It looks like something is on your mind. What's bothering you?" Sarah notices the expression on his face. "You can share it with me. I'm your girlfriend, you know..." She always shows such care for other's feelings.

Hearing her words, Jordan immediately brightens up. "It's because of the way you talk about Fraser. You really like him, don't you?" He cleverly changes the subject.

Sarah pauses, gathering courage.

"I once thought I might," she says. "I admired him deeply. And I wondered... if admiration and affection were the same thing. I let myself drift into that feeling for a little while."

She draws in a slow breath, steadying herself.

"But then I stood in front of Kelsi — saw her grace, her heart — and I knew I had to let that go. I watched him love her with his whole heart, and something in me settled — a truth I couldn't ignore. It wasn't my place to step into that. And it wasn't my story to chase."

Her eyes soften as she reaches for Jordan's hand.

"You are my story. You're where my heart rests when the world quiets down. And that's the love I want — the one that stays."

Jordan feels a quiet warmth spread through him. In all the years he's known her, she has never spoken with such honesty. He takes her hand in both of his, steady and grateful. When their eyes meet, he finds no trace of surprise — only a love they can finally name.

It's Saturday morning. Fraser just finished a tennis match with Jalen. Usually he finds himself on the losing side, but this time surprisingly he beats Jalen in three sets.

"Hey, how can you beat me? I doubt you've had time for coaching, so it must be AI training you," Jalen jokes over coffee as they sit down.

"You're half right. I used visual learning to study our past games and programmed myself to outplay you," Fraser replies, his wit as sharp as ever.

"Really?" Jalen recalls the report Fraser published and is well aware of his friend's intellectual capabilities.

"Hey, I'm just kidding," Fraser says as he takes a sip of coffee and a bite of a cinnamon roll. "I'm not quite at the level of programming that. Besides, that kind of application wouldn't be meaningful to me anyway. I'm focusing on something else."

"Not meaningful? You mean beating Djokovic is not meaningful?" Jalen continues jokingly. "When you're ready, sell me the program so I can become the number one player in the world. Tell me, what is meaningful to you?"

"I've developed a hat with goggles that can guide a blind child to walk safely, like the autopilot systems in smart cars," Fraser says with excitement. "Isn't this much more meaningful than winning a tennis match?"

"Oh, is that like the magic show you put on using visual learning? Kelsi mentioned it's more of a magic illusion than something real," Jalen says, finally touching the subject he's been curious about.

"It's not a magic illusion, Jalen. I initially wanted to use the performance as a humorous way to test my prototype, but it didn't go as planned," Fraser admits. He never hides anything from his best friend. "But it ended up exceeding my expectations. I love Kelsi very much, but I hadn't had the courage to tell her. And God gave me this chance." Although he knows Jalen isn't a Christian, Fraser never misses an opportunity to express his gratitude for what he sees as God's work.

Jalen looks impressed. "You know what, Fraser? A couple of weeks ago, my marketing manager came into my office with your backpack and told me about your research," he chuckles, continuing. "He doesn't know we're good friends and asked me to develop your research into marketable ideas. But when he opened the backpack, it was a stack of bibles. It is hilarious! I figured you'd never leave such an important invention at home, but you carried bibles that day."

"Is it Jordan who came to you? He's my friend's boyfriend. He might be a bit opportunistic, but he's okay," Fraser laughs, and he tells Jalen the story.

"Want to have another game? You used to be so hesitant on the tennis court, but today you hit every shot with confidence. "That's not like you. So, did Kelsi say yes to marrying you?" Jalen teases.

"No, I haven't proposed yet. Maybe I will after I finish my project," Fraser replies without any hesitation. "Actually, I'm feeling so good because my hat and goggles will finally help Charlie!"

"Is Charlie the blind kid you've been talking about? If your trial is successful, let me know so Sabrina and I can celebrate with you."

That night, after dinner, Kelsi is in Fraser's room chatting. Suddenly, Fraser takes her hand and guides her to the chair in front of the computer. With a mysterious smile, he says, "My love, I want you to try something. You need to close your eyes completely." He hands her an eyepatch.

Kelsi's heart starts pounding. "Is he going to propose to me with a ring?" she wonders, obediently putting on the eyepatch and sitting down.

She feels Fraser placing a hat on her head and adjusting the goggles over her eyes.

"I'm going to start the goggles on the count of three. Let's see if you can stand up and walk around without actually seeing," Fraser says warmly. "This is to test what I've made for Charlie tomorrow. One, two..."

Feeling a little disappointed, Kelsi stands up. A slight tingle behind her ears catches her attention as she takes a couple of steps forward. When she tries to take another step, she feels an invisible force guiding her to turn right. She walks a few steps, sensing Fraser's presence to the left behind the table. Navigating around, she finally runs into Fraser's arms.

"Wow, I can feel the surroundings without seeing!" she exclaims.

Fraser gently removes the hat, goggles, and eyepatch. "Tell me, how do you feel with the goggles on? Do you notice a strong current behind your ears? Does it hurt?"

"Something guided me to navigate without running into anything. I can't explain it, but the invisible guide feels real," Kelsi is amazed and almost at a loss for words. "The goggles are a bit heavy, but manageable. I felt just a slight tingling, but it wasn't uncomfortable at all."

Fraser looks up, raising the hat and goggles high, and whispers, "My Lord, the honor is Yours. Thank you for allowing me to serve You by turning my dream into reality. Blessed be Your name."

He turns around and hugs Kelsi tightly, their lips meeting in an unbroken kiss.

Chapter 7 *Children of Hope*

Achievement of the Impossible

The next morning, Fraser and Kelsi arrive at Maria's house, where Maria, Sarah, and Jordan are waiting. As they walk inside, Maria leads them to a table laden with churros, empanadas, and a fresh pot of coffee.

"Have some breakfast first; I made these this morning," Maria says enthusiastically as she pours two cups of coffee. They sit down, smiling at each other.

"I still haven't thanked you enough, Miss Kelsi," Maria says emotionally. "I don't know what I would have done without your help."

"We just came in at the right time," Kelsi replies. "If it weren't for Sarah, we wouldn't have known what had happened. It seems God sent me there that night," she says softly, this time from her heart.

As they talk, Fraser glances at the girl sitting in the wheelchair. Her shoulders slump forward, and her face has an eager expression, but she mutters incomprehensibly.

"Oh, it looks like Katie wants something to eat," he says, picking up a churro. He tears off a small piece and gently places it in her mouth.

Kelsi watches him tenderly. She never imagined the same hands always typing away at the keyboard could hold so much gentleness. And somehow, that quiet moment tells her more about him than all his inventions ever did.

Sarah comes out with Charlie, holding his hand without the cane. "Charlie is asleep, so I had to wake him up," she explains as she guides him to sit on a chair.

"Hi Charlie, I've brought you a new hat and glasses that can help you to walk. Do you feel excited?" Fraser says as he takes out the hat with goggles.

"Good morning, Uncle Fraser," Charlie politely replies as he recognizes Fraser's voice. Still muttering, he adds, "You are making me see!"

Fraser gently places the hat on Charlie's head. As he bends down to adjust the goggles to fit Charlie's eyes, Sarah feels a warmth rise in her chest. For a fleeting second, she imagines what it would be like if that tenderness were meant for her. The thought startles her. She quickly pushes it aside, ashamed of where her heart wants to wander. Fraser belongs with Kelsi — and she knows it. Still, she whispers a prayer, not for herself, but for the strength to rejoice in their love without letting envy steal her peace.

Fraser glances at Sarah. He catches the way her eyes soften, then steady, and wonders what prayers she carries in silence that he may never hear. Then his gaze shifts, and he finds Kelsi watching him, her gaze warm and unwavering. In that moment, he feels anchored, reminded that her love steadies him more than any prayer could.

Then he takes out his laptop and types for a minute.

"It should be fine now. Charlie, stand up slowly." He holds Charlie's hand steady. "Do you feel what's around you? Now walk a few steps."

Charlie hesitates for a second, then takes a step. "Keep walking, Charlie," Sarah's gentle voice encourages from ten feet away, standing behind a chair. "Come to me."

Charlie feels his hand in Fraser's, but there is no guiding movement. Hearing Sarah's voice, he senses her location and slowly walks toward her, going around the chair. It looks as if he is guiding Fraser instead.

"Charlie, come to me," Jordan's voice calls. He is standing fifteen feet away, next to Katie's wheelchair.

Charlie turns around slowly, pauses for a few seconds, and starts walking.

When he comes in front of the wheelchair, he stops and places his hand on Katie's face. After a second, he mutters again, "Sister..."

Everyone is moved, joyful tears welling up in their eyes, including Jordan's. His view of Fraser and his invention have completely changed. *"Now I understand why Sarah admires him. I admire him too,"* he murmurs to himself. Yet even as the words leave his lips, a knot forms in his chest. Admiration and envy collide — Fraser is everything he wants to be, and that truth burns.

As soon as Fraser lets go of Charlie's hand, Sarah steps forward and hugs him tightly. "You did it! Thank God for bringing you into our lives!" For Sarah, prayer is as natural as breathing — and in this moment, gratitude pours from her heart without effort.

With Sarah's warm body pressing against his, Fraser knows he would have reacted very differently just a few days ago. He feels the weight of her embrace, but more than that, the purity of her gratitude. He knows her words are meant for God as much as for him. So, he simply gives Sarah a quick, gentle squeeze before letting go. It isn't because Kelsi and Jordan are watching, but because his heart is filled with grace, and nothing else.

Fraser walks over to Maria and hands her a stack of papers. "Here is a brief explanation and the instructions for the hat and goggles, along with the charger."

He then walks to Charlie, giving him a warm hug and says, "Charlie, be a good boy. Uncle Fraser and Auntie Kelsi will come back to see you soon!" Turning to Maria and Sarah, his voice softens with quiet gratitude. "Thank you for trusting me with him. For the next week or so, don't let Charlie go out on the street alone until he's completely comfortable with the hat and goggles. This is my number. Please call me anytime — even just to tell me how he's doing. It would mean a lot to me."

Maria presses a hand to her chest, her eyes glistening. "We will. God bless you, Fraser," she whispers. Sarah nods beside her, unable to speak, her face shining with awe and relief. Kelsi's hand finds Fraser's arm, a proud smile spreading across her lips as if to say *this is why I love you*. Even Jordan, usually reserved, dips his head with quiet respect, the hint of a smile tugging at the corners of his mouth.

As Fraser and Kelsi are walking out, Jordan suddenly rushes over to them. "Fraser, is there anything I can do?"

Kelsi looks at him and senses his sincerity. A thought occurs to her. Before Fraser could respond, she interjects, "Jordan, could you make a video of Charlie to document his progress? A video demonstrating that blindness can be cured — there's immense value in that."

"Yes!" Jordan enthusiastically agrees. This is exactly what he needs to present to his boss. "Yes, I'll create a video showcasing Charlie wearing..."

"**Eyes of an Angel!**" Kelsi immediately jumps in, finishing his thought.

"He can walk with the **Eyes of an Angel**! That's truly a miracle!"

Fraser opens the car door for Kelsi to get in. Suddenly, he turns to Jordan. "Hey Jordan, could you please take videos of Katie in the wheelchair too, especially close-ups? I'd like to study her muscle and facial movements more closely so that I can collaborate with Drs. Johnson and Stephens to develop a program to assist Katie."

As they drive away, Sarah walks with Jordan to his car. Jordan suddenly stops.

"I need to tell you something, Sarah," he stutters. "That day when Fraser left his backpack, I didn't keep it. I took it to my boss at Alpha VC first." He takes a deep breath, regaining his composure. "I know it wasn't right, but I can't keep it from you. I wouldn't hide anything from you." His voice gains strength as he speaks with newfound courage.

Sarah's heart tightens. How could he betray someone's trust so easily? Anger flares — not just at what he did to Fraser, but at what it reveals about the man she's chosen. She wants to believe the best of him, yet doubt slips in like a shadow. What if she's been blind to his flaws all along?

"Why did you want to show his backpack to your boss?" she demands, her voice trembling with hurt. "Without his permission? He's a computer genius; he may have secrets inside. Jordan, you have to respect his privacy!" She pulls her hand from his, shaken by what she just heard.

Her words sting more than he expected. For the first time, Jordan wonders if her love is strong enough to see past his ambition — or if she's already begun to see him differently.

"I'm really sorry for what I did," Jordan says quietly, his eyes dropping to the ground.

"I thought he had the helmet and goggles you told me about in his bag. It would be valuable for our company to get familiar with them before the market does. But..."

"What did your boss say about it? I think nobody can understand those things except Fraser himself," Sarah asks, clearly quite unhappy.

"I found two bibles in the bag instead of the helmet and goggles," Jordan laughs dryly, "and my boss almost chewed me out."

Upon hearing that, Sarah chuckles. For the first time, she sees not just his mistake, but his courage in owning it. She gently takes his hand back and says softly, "See, God knows you aren't supposed to take someone else's bag, and He sent you a message." She doesn't know how the bibles ended up in Fraser's backpack instead of the helmet and goggles, but her words echo almost exactly what Fraser has said to Kelsi.

Jordan is deeply moved. He pulls Sarah into his arms and says," I understand now. God is watching over Fraser's noble acts and has been guiding and protecting him all along. God's real. After all these years, I never really listen to you, but I do now..."

Tears well in Sarah's eyes as she feels his arms tighten around her. All the years of distance and quiet disappointment melt away, replaced by a warmth she thought was long lost. For the first time in so long, she feels truly seen—not just by him, but for the quiet faith she's carried all along.

— ✦ —

Meanwhile, as Fraser is driving, he has his left hand gripping the steering wheel and right hand holding Kelsi's left hand tightly.

"I feel so excited," he says. "I watched Katie closely this morning. She has good control above her elbows, but little control from her lower arms to her fingers." He begins to describe what he saw in Katie, even though he knows Kelsi may not fully understand. "I notice she can't pronounce four syllables clearly and is probably mixing up words. Fortunately, her eyes are quite alert so her brain should be working well."

"That's good to know. So, can you use this observation to find a solution?" Kelsi asks, her voice full of hope.

"Not yet," Fraser replies. "When we get the video from Jordan, I'll watch it with the doctors and provide more details." He turns his head to look at Kelsi gently as he pulls his SUV to a stop in front of her dorm." I'll see you at dinner time." He gives her a kiss before driving away.

Kelsi walks back to her dorm, and suddenly she thinks of something. She hurries to her room and calls her dad.

"What's up, my baby?" Mr. Jiang's caring voice comes through the phone." Has Fraser done something to hurt you?"

"No, Dad, he's been wonderful to me. He's finally made a hat and goggles that help a blind kid sense their surroundings and walk on their own! I'm so excited!" Kelsi can't hide her excitement from her dad.

"Wow, that's incredible. I know his research has great potential. After you two get married, I'll help him start his own company to continue his research and explore other innovations," Mr. Jiang says, half-joking and half-serious.

"Marriage comes later, Dad. He has not proposed yet," Kelsi is not bashful in front of her dad." But I want to ask you something else. How do we patent his innovation device to protect his research and discovery?"

"Oh, you can talk with Mr. Ming Liu. He is on my patent team and he's the patent lawyer I always use. He should know you too. If he has any questions, ask him to call me."

It is Saturday again. Kelsi hasn't seen Fraser for two days because she has been busy writing her research paper, and Fraser has been occupied with meetings with two doctors and working on the AI program to align brainwaves with the human body with cerebral palsy. She misses him so much that she is about to call him for dinner.

Just then, she receives a call from her mother in Hong Kong.

"Hey, sweetie, Patrick just had a stroke and is now in the intensive care unit!" Mrs. Jiang immediately breaks the bad news, her voice cracking. Patrick is Kelsi's brother, ten years older but they are very close. He is also the executive manager of Mrs. Jiang's two restaurants.

Kelsi is shocked. "How can that be? Pat is only in his thirties! He's too young to have a stroke! How is he now?"

"He can't move or talk. This only happened a few hours ago, so we can't expect too much yet," Mrs. Jiang says, her voice trembling between worry and gratitude. "He collapsed in the restaurant kitchen, and a waiter saw him fell right away and called an ambulance. But on the way, the ambulance was stuck in a traffic jam caused by an accident. By the time they reached the hospital, the golden three-hour window had slipped away."

She tries to steady her voice, but the disappointment is clear. "He's receiving the best medical care possible right now. All we can do is hope and pray. By the time you come back in a few weeks, maybe he'll have regained some strength — but it won't be easy." Mrs. Jiang isn't a Christian, but in distress— even a successful businesswoman finds herself resorting to prayer.

After Kelsi hangs up the phone, she immediately calls Fraser, needing someone to share her emotions with. The phone rings and rings, but Fraser is not answering.

It's the first time Fraser hasn't picked up her call. Ever since they exchanged phone numbers in the cafeteria, Fraser has always answered within five seconds — even when he's in the shower.

What's happening to him? This isn't like him! She starts to worry. *Could he be sick? But he always lets me know. Maybe someone stole his phone so he can't answer? No, he's so careful. Could he have a stroke?* Suddenly, she shudders. *No, he's only twenty-six... but Pat has a stroke too...* She can't bear her thoughts and rushes to his apartment in her BMW.

Security greets her at the front door of the apartment building. "Bill, I've been trying to reach Fraser, and he hasn't answered." She explains urgently. "Can I go up to his room to check on him? I need to make sure he's alright."

Bill, who has seen Fraser and Kelsi together intimately for a while, trusts her concern and escorts her to Fraser's room.

When Bill opens the door, they find Fraser's room empty, with the helmet and goggles missing.

As they descend the stairs, Bill suggests, "Maybe you should check nearby hospitals to see if he had an accident?" He is not very tactful.

"Yes, I should. Thank you, Bill," Kelsi replies quietly. She walks slowly to her BMW, struggling to accept the idea that Fraser might be in a hospital.

"Where could he be?" she wonders aloud, tears in her eyes. She has never imagined she could miss someone so intensely besides her parents.

Then, unexpectedly, she considers going to the church to pray. She has never prayed before. Yet love leads her here, to words she does not know, searching for a God she is just beginning to seek.

After parking her BMW, she makes her way to the prayer room.

Chapter 8 *An Uneasy Rescue*

Undercover Angel Encounter

That afternoon, Fraser drives to Maria's home to see Charlie and Katie. He is very pleased to see Charlie quickly learning to walk with the aid of the Eyes of an Angel. He also takes some notes on how Katie's facial expressions respond to his voice, and how her lower limbs move in coordination with her upper body. Afterward, he waves goodbye to Maria and leaves.

Due to road construction, he has parked his SUV two blocks away. As he walks toward his car, a man in a black jacket and hoodie approaches him and pulls out a knife.

"Give me your wallet or else," the man threatens.

Fear pricks, but instinct answers first. Knowing it is unwise to fight someone with a knife, Fraser slowly pulls out his wallet, throws it hard in the opposite direction, and runs like mad toward his SUV. He hopes the man would go after the wallet, giving him time to get into his car and drive away.

Leaving the wallet on the street, the hoodlum reaches his car just a step ahead of him. "Give me your backpack too," he demands, moving closer and pointing the 7-inch army knife at Fraser.

If it is anything else, Fraser would have surrendered his backpack. But it contains his computer, which holds all his research materials and more. He couldn't give it up, not even to save his own life.

He takes a couple of steps back, his mind racing. "Should I fight him? Can I beat him? Or should I run with my backpack? Can he catch me? What if I give him the backpack and he still wants to hurt me?" He didn't have time to pray.

Seeing no response, the hoodlum steps forward, grabbing a corner of the backpack with his left hand and stabbing Fraser in the chest with his right. "Let go!" he yells.

Though Fraser doesn't know martial arts, he is quite athletic from playing a lot of tennis. He quickly pulls the backpack in front of him to block the knife, shifting his body in the process. The knife slips, slicing his left arm, but he successfully pulls back his backpack from the hoodlum.

Blood begins seeping through his shirt.

The hoodlum is visibly upset. He lunges forward, trying to stab Fraser again. Fraser darts to the other side of his SUV, but the door won't open; his fingers fumble on the handle, slick with fear.

The hoodlum charges after him, knife raised.

But before he can reach Fraser, a strong hand clamps down on his knife-wielding right arm.

He jerks back in shock, trying to twist free, but the grip forces his arm upward. The knife slips from his hand and clatters onto the pavement.

"Jordan! You come just in time!" Fraser shouts, breathless with relief and disbelief.

For a split second he just stares, stunned that help arrives at the exact moment he needs it most.

This can't be just a coincidence.

"Thank You, Lord…" his heart whispers. *"I don't know how You do it, but You always send the right angel when I need one most."*

He knows—this rescue isn't luck. It is grace arriving in the hands of a friend.

Jordan, initially facing the other way, turns around, nods, and pulls out his phone with his free hand to dial 911. Still holding the mugger's arm, he asks, "Fraser, is that you? What are you doing here alone? This isn't a very safe neighborhood. Is Kelsi with you?" His concern is evident in his voice.

"No, Kelsi is working on her paper. I came to check on Charlie and Katie. Are you here to see Sarah?" Fraser asks.

"Sarah is at church. I just came to take more videos of Charlie and Katie," Jordan replies.

As they speak, a police car arrives. Jordan hands over the mugger, and they follow the police to the station, file a report, and have Fraser's arm treated.

As they leave the station, Jordan says," Maybe you should call Kelsi and tell her about this."

"Let me stop by the church to thank God first. If I call Kelsi now, she'll worry sick and want to see me immediately. I can always see her later tonight."

Since Fraser left his SUV near Maria's house, Jordan drives him to the church to meet Sarah.

As Kelsi enters the prayer room, she sees Fraser gazing at the cross and whispering, " Thank You, Lord. In every moment of need, You send angels my way. Blessed be Your name."

She dashes over and wraps her arms around Fraser's neck. "Where have you been, Fritz? I've been so worried about you!" Fraser turns to her, hugs her tightly, and says, "Somehow, I knew you'd be here. I met another angel today."

Then Kelsi notices Sarah and Jordan standing near the back of the prayer room, smiling warmly at them. The sacred light of the cross, glowing faintly under the moonlight streaming through the high window, casts a gentle radiance across their faces. One by one, they draw closer until the four of them stand together, hands linked in a quiet circle of gratitude.

Fraser's voice trembles with emotion. "I owe my life to you, Jordan. I was attacked near my car, and you appeared at the very moment I needed help most."

Jordan shakes his head. "I just happened to be there, filming the kids at Maria's house. When I saw what was happening, I ran in and called 911. I didn't even realize it was you until afterward."

Kelsi reaches for Fraser's hand. "I called you again and again," she says softly. "When you didn't answer, something inside told me to come here. I didn't even think—I just drove."

Then Sarah bows her head, her voice gentle yet sure. "Oh Lord, how can we thank You for Your guidance? You placed each of us exactly where we needed to be—one to protect, one to comfort, one to witness Your grace. You are our Lord. Amen."

For a moment, the room is still. Only the silver light on the cross moves, shifting softly with the night breeze. Fraser exhales, his heart full. As they rise, Kelsi turns to Fraser. "Before we go get your SUV," she says softly, "let's stop for coffee. I think we both need to breathe a little."

Fraser nods, smiling faintly. "Starbucks?"

She nods back. "Starbucks."

— ✦ —

"I can do anything with a computer, but I'm useless against a guy pointing a knife at me," Fraser chuckles, taking a sip of coffee. Then, looking at Jordan, he adds with a grin, "The way you took down that guy — are you a black belt or something!"

"Oh yes, he's a Taekwondo black belt!" Sarah proudly answers for Jordan. "He's been protecting me from bullies since middle school. He's always been my hero!" She wraps her hand around his arm and flashes that lovely smile.

Jordan's face turns a little red; he's never good with words. But Sarah continues, "Remember the day Charlie had the accident? He lost so much blood, and the hospital was running dangerously low that night. The doctors weren't sure how long he could hold on. Jordan didn't even wait to be asked — he rolled up his sleeve and gave two pints on the spot, against the doctor's suggestion of only one. That's what kept Charlie alive. He's a hero to Maria's family." She wraps her hands around his neck.

Kelsi and Fraser are amazed at what she said. Based on what they know of him, they can't imagine him performing such an act. Fraser winks at Jordan showing appreciation and approval.

Jordan's face turns even redder, and he is left speechless.

Kelsi pulls her BMW to a stop beside Fraser's SUV. During the drive, she has told him about her brother's stroke in Hong Kong. Before Fraser can open the door, she reaches across and takes his left hand, her voice trembling.

"What if my brother doesn't recover? Could he be paralyzed for life? He's only thirty-four!" she cries, her eyes glistening with fear and helplessness.

Fraser turns toward her, his tone calm but heavy with concern. "It depends on the type of stroke he had," he says gently. "Most strokes, if treated within the crucial three-hour window, have about an eighty-five percent chance of recovery. But because the ambulance was delayed, that window closed before doctors could begin treatment. I know that's heartbreaking to hear, and I wish I could tell you otherwise."

Tears slip down Kelsi's cheeks. "Why does everything fall apart at once?" she whispers. "I can handle work, stress, anything — but not this. Not losing him."

Fraser watches her struggle for words, his heart aching at the sight. "Kelsi," he says softly, "I know how helpless it feels when someone you love is hurting. But right now, your brother needs your prayers more than your fear. Let's keep believing that God hasn't finished His work yet."

He reaches across the passenger seat, lifting her chin tenderly. "Whatever happens, we'll face this together," he whispers, pressing a soft, reassuring kiss to her lips. "You're not alone in this."

The promise steadies her more than the facts ever could.

Several days later, Kelsi calls Fraser." Fritz, I just finished my paper, and I am going home to see my brother," she says, her voice trembling with worry. "My mom says the doctors haven't seen any improvement in him these past few days," she's about to cry.

"Oh, that's awful. When are you leaving? I will come with you, Kelsi," Fraser replies, eager to support her during this difficult time.

"I'd love for you to come too, Fritz, but you need to finish the Eyes of an Angel prototype to help Katie," Kelsi says, calming down slightly, though she still feels concerned. "I booked the earliest flight I could, for Thursday. Today's Monday, so I have a couple of days to turn in my paper and talk with my professor."

After a brief pause, she adds, "If you can make it, I'll add another passenger to my booking."

"Yes, please do, Kelsi. I'll wrap things up and go with you," Fraser replies.

Knowing Fraser would be with her back home, Kelsi feels a sense of sweetness and peace, allowing her to sleep soundly that night.

However, Fraser could not find the same peace. He twists and turns in his bed, his mind racing with concern for Kelsi. He cares about her so much that he wants to ease her worries in every possible way.

"Why does recovery become so difficult once the golden window is missed?" Fraser asks himself, pacing the room.

Then it clicks. "I've been working on brainwaves for cerebral palsy patients. Could this same approach be applied to stroke patients who are beyond the treatment window? There must be some overlap. If I can help Katie, maybe I can help Patrick too!"

A surge of excitement courses through him. He leaps out of bed and hurries straight to his computer, determination burning in his eyes.

— ✦ —

Come Thursday evening, Sabrina takes Fraser and Kelsi to the airport.

"Jalen is in China right now. I've told him and he'll visit Patrick when he's back in Hong Kong," Sabrina says as she walks them to the gate." How long are you guys staying? Maybe Jalen can meet up with you both too before you leave."

"We're not sure. It depends on how Patrick is doing and how urgently Fritz needs to return for his research," Kelsi answers softly, setting down her carry-on.

Sabrina turns to Fraser, who looks pale and exhausted. It seems he has not been sleeping for a couple of days.

"Hey, take it easy. The honeymoon hasn't even started," she always likes to tease him whenever she can. But Fraser is just resting his hand on Kelsi's shoulder, silently smiling.

"Gosh, this is the most stressful honeymoon I've ever seen!" Sabrina continues, trying to lighten the mood with her joviality.

"Not sure... we haven't seen yours yet..." Fraser finally jabs back with a smile. "Believe me, when our real honeymoon comes, it will be nothing like this."

— ✦ —

Fraser is sitting next to Kelsi in the Business Class section of the airplane. It is the first time he has travelled with Kelsi, and also the first time he sits in business class.

"I'm glad you made the reservation. If it is up to me, I'd be in economy," Fraser blurts out sincerely, then immediately regrets. "What did I just say? She's a billionaire's daughter. I shouldn't keep bringing this up..." he mutters to himself.

But Kelsi doesn't seem to be upset. "I'll be with you wherever you are, economy or not. For long trips, business class is a little more comfortable though," she responds softly.

"But in these seats, it's hard to hold your hand..." Feeling the size of the seats and the comfortable separation, his wit comes back.

Kelsi reaches out and grabs Fraser's hand. "Yes, it's a little tricky but still doable," she pretends to be serious, but couldn't help laughing together.

The flight attendant arrives and places drinks on their trays.

Kelsi turns to Fraser and asks," Fritz, you look exhausted. Have you finished what you are working on? I want you to relax with me for these few days." She then remembers Sabrina's comment. "Let's make this a pre-honeymoon," she whispers shyly.

Then she realizes that Fraser has leaned back, his eyes closed, and is softly snoring. She gets up, grabs a blanket and gently places it over him.

Chapter 9 *Transworld Healing*

A Second-Time Miracle

It's a long flight. Even though Fraser spends most of the time sleeping, Kelsi still manages to chat with him every now and then.

"You're exhausted. You must have burned the midnight oil finishing Katie's Eyes of an Angel," Kelsi remarks, knowing him well enough to understand that once he starts something, he won't stop until it is done.

"That's almost finished. I'm working on something else now. By the way, would it be alright if I stay at a hotel instead of your home?" Fraser asks hesitantly. He knows Kelsi might be upset, but he's not comfortable with the butlers, chauffeurs, and maids he is sure they have in their mansion.

"No, you're staying at my house," home, she means—whether he hears it or not. "Unless you have a very good reason," Kelsi continues with a smile on her face. "Like sneaking out to see your other girlfriends," she adds, clearly having spent enough time with Fraser to adopt his sense of humor.

"You know I love spending every day with you, Kelsi," Fraser says, choosing his words carefully. "But it might not be the right time for me to meet all your relatives. We aren't even engaged yet. Plus, I need some time alone to do some research that might help Patrick." He skillfully shifts the topic to something she cares about.

Upon hearing these words from Fraser, Kelsi immediately brightens. She knows he wouldn't hint at a promise unless he is sure he can keep it. She doesn't need to ask for details; she trusts him completely.

"But my mom really wants you to stay with us," she says, looking at Fraser with hopeful eyes.

"Helping Patrick is more important. You can tell her I'll come by soon to let her test my culinary skills," Fraser replies, ending the conversation with another promise — one he is eager to keep.

When they step out of the gate, Fraser sees Kelsi's mom waiting with a teenage girl. Kelsi rushes to her mom, hugging her and yelling,"Hi, Mom!" The girl hurries to Kelsi, grabs her carry-on, and says, "Hi, sis."

Kelsi then hugs the girl, looks her up and down, and says," You've gotten so tall! Hey, Fraser, meet my mom and my sister, Britney."

With a smile, Fraser immediately steps forward, hugs Kelsi's mom, and says, "Hi, Auntie." Then he extends his hand to the girl. "Hi, Britney, I'm Fraser, your sister's good friend."

"My sister has a lot of good friends, but you're probably her best friend," Britney responds mischievously, giving Fraser a firm handshake.

As they walk toward Mrs. Jiang's minivan, Kelsi asks her mom, "Can you drop Fraser off at the Sheraton first? He needs to stay there for a few days for an AI conference." She carefully explains why Fraser wouldn't be staying at their house.

"Oh, of course. Business comes first," Mrs. Jiang says, giving an understanding smile. Then, looking at Fraser, she adds, "But you have to come and stay with us once you're done."

Fraser feels relieved; he needs a few days to unwind and finish his AI simulation work.

After Kelsi settles into her room, Britney comes in and sits on her sister's bed. "Hey sis, Fraser seems cool. You mentioned he's a computer genius. How did you find him? You never liked computers much, just like me."

"Actually, he found me," Kelsi says with a smile. "He sat across from me in the cafeteria and introduced himself. It surprised me a bit because computer nerds usually aren't that sociable." Kelsi is mesmerized by the memory. "But he's so funny and caring..."

"He's much more decent than Peter, Larry, Richard, George..." Britney says, laughing as she counts Kelsi's past friends." They are all spoiled rotten freaks..."

"You know Fritz makes great pastries too!" Kelsi beams with pride when she talks about Fraser. "I'll ask him to make your favorite banana bread. It is out of this world!"

"Are we talking about Fraser's cooking?" Mrs. Jiang steps in with a smile. "Your sister gets so excited every time she mentions him. I'll invite him to cook a meal for us when he's free. Now, it's dinner time, girls."

Meanwhile, Fraser is lying on the bed, typing his thoughts into the laptop when the phone rings.

"Hey Fritz, we're visiting Patrick tomorrow. Can we pick you up at 10, have brunch, and then head over?" Kelsi seems more assertive when she is at home.

"Certainly. Who's joining us?" Fraser asks.

"Just my mom and Britney," Kelsi replies." I only have two siblings. Pat is ten years older, but Britney is seven years younger. There's quite a big age gap between us, which is pretty unusual. But we are very close."

"Oh, I'm actually the youngest in my family," Fraser says, with a touch of sadness in his tone. "I've been a nerd all my life and have had trouble communicating with my siblings, so I ended up spending a lot of time alone doing my own thing. I often wished I had a younger brother or sister to play with." He sighs softly.

"But you communicate so well now!" Kelsi jumps in. "You're so witty and caring that sometimes I forget you're a computer scientist. What changed your life? Is it because of a girl?" She adds playfully.

"Yes and no. Kelsi, I haven't shared with you much about my past, but I will now," Fraser begins. "I fell in love with a girl in college. Seemed we like each other a lot, but I am too shy to commit," he says softly, as if lost in a dream. "Before we graduated, she met someone else and told me she was getting engaged. She hinted that if I want to continue our relationship, I need to take action." He sighs. "I am too shy and so uncertain of the future, I let her go."

"Then what happened?" Kelsi asks, showing her curiosity. The Fraser she knows is outspoken and assertive, not shy and reserved.

"I was very depressed during that time," Fraser continues. "I withdrew from everything for a year. Then I joined a bible study group and started going to church, and that changed my life." If Kelsi is here in person, he would surely give her a warm embrace.

"Gradually, I became much more focused on my work and started having inspirations I couldn't explain. The pastor assigned me to lead a cell group, and since then, my communication skills have drastically improved."

Kelsi is deeply touched. "Do I remind you of your previous girlfriend?" She asks with a light smile.

"No — you don't look anything like her at all," Fraser says, pausing briefly. "Looking back, I see that we weren't really compatible. But love doesn't always follow rhyme or reason." He sighs. "When I met you, something inside me told me you were my angel — and I should never let you go."

"Where is she now? Can I meet her someday?" Kelsi asks, tilting her head.

Fraser raises his eyebrows, unsure if she's teasing or serious. He replies with light humor, "You can meet her if she happens to be in the same hospital where Patrick is staying. But no — I have no idea where she is now."

— ✦ —

In the hospital, Kelsi, Fraser, Mrs. Jiang and Britney all stand beside Patrick's bed. A therapist is helping Patrick to sit up, while a doctor observes.

"No, he isn't responding," the therapist says to the doctor. "His left upper arm shows a little movement, but not his back or feet."

The doctor gestures them to follow him as they walk outside.

"Patrick has severe heart blockage in addition to the clots in his brain," Dr. Lau explains to the family. "His brain isn't getting enough oxygen to control his body, making his recovery very challenging."

"It could be his diet and lack of exercise," Mrs. Jiang says sadly. "Pat loves to eat and doesn't watch what he eats, and he works in restaurants. What should we do now?"

"I recommend a coronary artery bypass graft within the next couple of days to strengthen his heart first, followed by a thrombectomy to remove the remaining stroke clots," Dr. Lau gently suggests. After a brief pause, he continues, "These procedures can be done within four to five days, but it's ultimately up to our Lord to give him the strength to regain his movement and speech abilities." It seems Dr. Lau is a Christian too.

"I agree, let's do it," Mrs. Jiang says decisively, displaying the confidence of a successful businesswoman. "I need to return to the two restaurants now that Pat is away. You all may stay with him for a while. If you like, you can have dinner outside. I know you three want to chat."

After she left, Kelsi, Fraser, and Britney return to Patrick's room. Patrick looks at them, eager to speak, but no words come out.

Fraser approaches him and holds both of his hands, studying Patrick's face. Then he leans in, close enough to read his lips. After a few seconds, he looks up and notices the cross hanging above Patrick's bed.

He kneels and whispers a prayer, his voice barely above a breath.

Kelsi and Britney watch, unable to hear what he says.

After a moment, Fraser rises again, still gazing at the cross.

"What is he doing?" Britney whispers, tugging gently at Kelsi's arm.

"He's praying," Kelsi says softly, placing a hand on her sister's shoulder.

"Every time he does that... he's about to perform miracles." She watches Fraser with loving eyes. "I'll explain later."

As they step out of the hospital, Fraser notices the minivan still there." Did Auntie take the minivan?" He wonders and asks.

"No, she left the car for us to use for the rest of the day. She took Uber to her restaurant," Kelsi smiles as she opens the car door.

"Uber? Isn't your chauffeur picking her up?" Fraser asks, surprises.

"We don't have a chauffeur, Fritz, we drive our own cars," Kelsi speaks as she starts the engine. "My dad has chauffeurs for the company, but we like to drive ourselves at home. Why do you look so surprised?"

Fraser is speechless.

Kelsi and Britney entertain Fraser with a sightseeing tour.

"How long have you been away from Hong Kong, Fritz? I heard sis keeps calling you Fritz. Can I call you Fritz too?" Britney asks Fraser innocently.

"Of course, Britney," Fraser smiles. "I left fifteen years ago. I spent my last couple of high school years in the States." As he gazes out the car window, he exclaims, "Wow, this place had changed so much I can hardly recognize it anymore. I used to get street food right here, and now it's a high-rise!" He points to a spot outside.

They stop at a quiet bistro for dinner.

After ordering, Britney turns to Fraser again. "Sis told us you're very good with computers, but why is it so difficult for me?"

"Computer is a very strange subject, Brit. You either get it or you don't," Fraser says, taking a sip of tea. "For me, I don't need much teaching. I read and understand. But it's different for everyone. Each person has their own unique talents." He points to Kelsi and continues, "Your sister has musical and artistic talents I never had..."

"But you can pretend you have them using your AI thing," Kelsi cheerfully interrupts.

"What's that?" Britney asks, confused.

"I'll tell you the story later," Kelsi smiles as she holds Fraser's hand under the table.

As they ate, Fraser glances at Britney. "So Brit, you're in college prep now. Have you thought about what comes after graduation? Staying here to help your parents, or maybe studying abroad?"

Britney sets her fork down, her expression thoughtful. "I've been thinking about it a lot. They haven't said anything directly, but... I can tell they'd like me to stay and help with the family business." She pauses, then adds quietly," It's just the three of us now."

Kelsi chimes in, her voice soft and uncertain. "I studied business too, but..." She cast a brief glance at Fraser, then at Britney. "I'm not sure how much help I can be to Mom and Dad. I know business is never really your thing," she says with a faint smile." I just hope Pat's recovery keeps going well. The stroke really shook us."

— ✦ —

A few days later, Fraser and the Jiang family are back at the hospital. They sit in the waiting room, anxiously watching the door to the operating room.

The door opens, and Dr. Lau steps out with a smile. "The operations are very successful," he announces. "Let him rest for a few hours, and then you can see him."

Everyone takes turns shaking hands with Dr. Lau and expressing their gratitude.

Just like last time, Mrs. Jiang leaves for the restaurant quickly, while Kelsi, Britney, and Fraser stay behind.

"Let's sit down, relax, and have some coffee before coming back here," Fraser suggests." I have something very important to tell you both."

They choose a nearby Starbucks and settle down. Fraser opens his backpack and pulls out a hat attached to a pair of goggles.

Kelsi immediately exclaims, "Eyes of an Angel!" She stands up and grabs Fraser by both arms, clearly very excited.

97

Britney picks up the hat. She has been hearing stories from her sister over the past few days and is amazed by what her soon-to-be brother-in-law could do. Now she finally gets to see the Eyes of an Angel. "How does it work?" she asks.

Fraser calmly sits them down. "Later today when we get back to Pat's room, I'll run a little test first, but you two have to help me." He tries to explain as clearly as he could.

"A few days ago when we visited him, I noticed he had not lost his hearing. He could speak in a very low tone, almost inaudible," Fraser says, pointing to the tiny wire attached to the hat." So I added a mic to amplify his voice, but I couldn't find a speaker small enough to attach. His voice has to be listened to through the computer."

Before Britney could say "wow", Fraser adds, "But his voice is very muffled. I have to filter it before it can be understood." He picks up the goggles and continues." These goggles will translate what he sees into brainwaves that instruct his muscles to perform. Hopefully his brain power is strong enough to direct his body."

"Oh, that's what you used for your church magic show? So this is tested and it has to work, right?" Britney asks anxiously.

"No, there is a major difference. I can control my body movements, but he can't. He's lost his muscle memory to do that," Fraser says seriously. "So, you two have to help me out. He doesn't know me, so whatever I say and do won't mean much to him." He hugs each sister with one of his arms. "But you are his beloved sisters, and he knows and trusts you. So,

98

talk to him, get him to look at you, and perform simple hand movements so he can follow. He has to have the will to do it, and only you both can help him discover that will."

What he means is that he can guide Patrick how to move — but only his sisters can give him the reason to try.

Each of them picks up their paper cup and drinks it to the bottom. Then Fraser claps his hands and says, "Let's go do it!"

"You sound just like my mom," Britney quips, and they all laugh.

Chapter 10 *A Feast of Love*

Bonding with Heart and Soul

A few weeks later, they are back at the hospital — this time in the cafeteria, chatting with Dr. Lau while Patrick works with his therapist on hand-eye coordination.

"Miracles happen every day!" Dr. Lau says, his voice filled with wonder. Today, the word doesn't feel like exaggeration. "Patrick has made progress unlike anything I've seen in my career." He looks at Fraser intently.

"You've been visiting him so faithfully these past weeks, and now he's following instructions, feeding himself, even speaking much more clearly. What have you done? And what is that helmet and those goggles you've put on him?"

Then recognition lights up his eyes. "Wait — is that the *Eyes of an Angel* I've read about?"

"Yes — my brother is being healed by the *Eyes of an Angel!*" Britney exclaims, her voice trembling with gratitude.

Dr. Lau's warm laugh sounds like science smiling. Knowing Fraser's background in computer science and his quiet faith, he senses something divine behind Patrick's healing.

Fraser smiles humbly and takes Kelsi's hand. "It's all for the glory of God," he says. "The *Eyes of an Angel* helped, yes — but it's their love and patience that made the real difference." He looks at Kelsi and Britney with gentle pride. "Technology can train the mind, but only care can reach the heart. What you've both done for Patrick — that's what healing truly is."

Kelsi's eyes glisten as she squeezes Fraser's hand, her voice barely a whisper. "Amen to that."

Mrs. Jiang keeps gazing at Fraser. Gratitude finds what money cannot name.

As they step out of the hospital, she turns to him with a playful smile. "You owe us a home-cooked meal. Come tomorrow — we'll see how good you really are." Her smile seems to gather all three of them into its warmth.

"Come, let's do it!" Britney mimics her mother's voice, and everyone bursts into laughter.

The next day, Kelsi drives Fraser to the supermarket to pick up his ingredients. "We have all the utensils, seasonings and spices. You just pick your meats and vegetables," Kelsi says, smiling," and Britney can create a YouTube video."

"I've never cooked in someone else's kitchen before," Fraser admits nervously. *Their kitchen is probably bigger than most restaurants. What if I mess this up?*

Kelsi drives through an electronic gate, past a small flower garden, and parks in front of a large two-story house. They each carry bags of groceries as they walk inside.

"Oh, you're finally here!" Mrs. Jiang and Britney exclaim as they see them coming in, rushing over to help carry their bags. "Come, follow me into the kitchen," Mrs. Jiang says.

Aside from Mrs. Jiang and Britney, Fraser doesn't see anyone else around. He whispers into Kelsi's ear, "Did your maids and butlers take the day off?"

"What maids and butlers? We don't have any," Kelsi replies, giggling at Fraser's surprise. "The cleaning ladies come once a week, but today isn't their day. There are only five of us living here—Mom, Dad, Pat, Britney, and me. Do you really think we had a bunch of servants?"

"But..." Fraser is speechless as Kelsi continues, "Just because we can afford something doesn't mean we need it. My parents have always taught us to take care of ourselves. Now start your preparation. Britney and I will help you, but you have to help us with the dishes later." She adds cheerfully.

Fraser wants to hold her in his arms and kiss her, but he has to save it for later.

At the dining table, Britney picks up a piece of curry chicken. "This is one of my favorite dishes," she says, taking a bite. "Wow—so tender, and the spice is perfect. I watch you make it, but I have no idea how you got it this good!" She takes another bite, shaking her head in amazement.

"Curried chicken isn't just curry powder —you need turmeric and garam masala too," Fraser explains, warming to his subject. "I use only dark meat with bones, boiling it over medium-low heat for only ten minutes. The secret is to let it sit covers for another five minutes." He became visibly excited as he talks about cooking, just as much as he is about computers.

Mrs. Jiang takes a bite of the steamed fish and says, "It's very tender, but not undercooked. Both my restaurant chefs could never cook it like this." She turns to Fraser with admiration. "You timed it perfectly!"

"Restaurant chefs often oversteam fish because they have to be sure it's cooked through," Fraser replies, brightening. "Fish is easily overcooked. The timing really depends on the size and texture. For larger fish, I always make a couple of slices to expose the bones. And the real secret—" he lowers his voice playfully, "—is letting it sit covered for three to four minutes after turning off the heat."

Kelsi and Britney exchange impressed looks; his knowledge of steaming fish surprises even them.

After dinner, Fraser serves them banana bread.

Britney takes a bite, then rushes over to give him a hug. "This is the best banana bread I've ever tasted! Sis must have told you it's my favorite!"

Fraser laughs softly and gently pulls away. "It's a bit different because I use almond and coconut flour, avocado oil, and maple syrup instead of regular flour, butter, and white sugar. It's healthier, too."

Britney nods vigorously, still chewing. "I don't care what's in it — just keep making it *exactly* like this."

Kelsi chuckles, shaking her head. "Brit only cares about taste. If Fritz baked it with rocket fuel, she'd still eat it."

Britney shrugs proudly. "Only if it tastes this good."

After dinner, Fraser and the two girls start clearing the table and washing the dishes. There are too many to fit in the dishwasher, so they hand-wash most of them. He can hardly believe he's standing here at the sink, washing dishes with a billionaire's two daughters.

When they finish, Britney heads back to her room to chat with her friends online, while Kelsi leads Fraser on a quiet tour of the house.

"This is the living room… this is the office… this is the office… this is the library… this is my parents' room… this is Pat's room… and this is Britney's room…"

Finally, they arrive at her own door. They step inside, and she quietly closes it behind them.

Without a word, they move into each other's arms, and their lips meet with an urgency they've both been holding back.

"I've missed you so much these past few days," Kelsi murmurs against his chest. "I know you've been busy perfecting the *Eyes of an Angel* for Pat... thank God it works. We wouldn't have known what to do without you. There are some things money just can't buy."

"I had a brother who died of a stroke and a heart attack," Fraser says softly, running his hand through her hair. "That was three years ago, and I promised myself I'd do everything I could to stop that from happening to others." He pauses. "I'm not a medical doctor, but... it feels like God has given me another kind of calling."

Kelsi looks up and loops her arms around his neck. "A few of my exes called this week. Word gets around fast."

"They asked you out? How dare they! I'll get Jordan to handle them," Fraser says, trying to sound serious but already laughing.

"No need. Britney already took care of it. She told them I'm engaged," Kelsi says, laughing with her.

"Oh, you are? To anyone I know?" Fraser teases—but the moment he sees Kelsi's eyes, quiet and searching, his smile fades.

Suddenly she asks, "Do you like Sarah? Don't lie to me."

Fraser freezes, blindsided.

"No man on earth wouldn't like her," Kelsi says, her voice trembling slightly. "And I think she likes you too. But when you told me about having dinner with her—when you didn't hide it—I realized you're different. Real love keeps no secrets." Tears slip from her eyes as she looks at him.

"I did like Sarah," Fraser admits gently, brushing her tears away. "I was confused for a while. But one night during prayer, I realized God wanted me to focus on helping others, not worrying about my love life. He would lead me where I was meant to be."

He takes her face in his hands. "And He led me to you. You are my destiny, Kelsi."

And in that moment, he finally sees her not as a billionaire's daughter, but as the warm, thoughtful girl he has been falling in love with all along.

She breathes out slowly, her forehead resting against his. "I guess it's true... if you love something, set it free. If it comes back, it's yours..."

Time seems to stop as they hold each other close.

The next morning, as they are having breakfast, Fraser stands up and looks at Mrs. Jiang.

"Auntie, I'd like to ask for Kelsi's hand in marriage," Fraser says, his voice steady despite his racing heart. The courage feels simple; the moment is anything but.

Not at all surprised, Mrs. Jiang smiles. "Fraser, where's the romance? Why propose over breakfast?" she teases.

Kelsi and Britney exchange glances, waiting for his answer.

"Well, I asked my AI assistant when I should propose," Fraser says, miming typing on his laptop. "It said, 'If you can't live without each other, what are you waiting for?'" He shrugs. "So... here I am."

Everyone bursts into laughter.

Then Mrs. Jiang raises a hand. "You have my blessing — but on one very important condition." She pauses deliberately, making all of them lean in.

"You must agree to share the secrets of your curried chicken and banana bread with our restaurant chefs, so I can put them on the menu."

This time, everyone laughs even harder.

— ✦ —

Three months later, in the chapel at Tri-City Church.

Fraser stands at the altar with Jalen and Jordan flanking him. Over a hundred guests fill the chapel. He has given presentations to larger crowds, but today his hands tremble slightly as he adjusts his tie.

"Can't believe you beat us to it, Fraser," Jalen says with a smile, giving his best friend a friendly pat on the shoulder.

If not us, then who... If not me and you...

The Matthew West lyrics run through Fraser's mind — the song that changed everything for him.

Jordan keeps glancing anxiously down the aisle.

The chapel doors open as the music starts.

Sarah enters, bouquet in hand, walking gracefully with a bright smile. When her eyes meet Jordan's, her gaze locks onto him. She steps to his side and slips her hand around his arm.

Sabrina follows, also carrying a bouquet, greeting the guests with warm smiles before her eyes settle on Jalen. She moves beside him and gently wraps her hand around his arm.

After a brief pause, a hush falls over the chapel.

A girl in a wheelchair quietly enters the aisle, a bouquet clutched in her left hand while her right guides her chair forward with steady determination.

Behind her walks a boy, a basket held in his left hand as he confidently scatters rose petals on both sides of the aisle.

For a moment, no one breathes. Some in the audience have seen children like them before — girls who once could barely move on their own, boys who never met anyone's eyes. Now, watching these two move with grace and confidence, they can't help but feel they are witnessing something — something extraordinary, something divine.

108

No one pays attention to their clothing; all eyes are drawn to the hats and goggles they wear — each marked with the *Eyes of an Angel* logo, softly gleaming under the chapel lights.

At the altar, Fraser steadies himself, his chest tightening with pride and humility as he watches the children.

Sarah, still holding her bouquet, presses it against her heart, her eyes glistening with tears.

For a moment, the entire chapel seems united in awe and gratitude.

When the two children reach the altar, a woman steps forward and extends both hands to guide them to one side. Her eyes brim with joyful tears. "Thank you, Mr. Fraser," she whispers, her voice breaking. "For giving them a new life."

Fraser remains silent. His gaze stays fixed on Katie and Charlie. He looks up, his heart swelling with gratitude — for the calling he serves, and for the blessings he has received in return.

The bridal march starts playing. Kelsi has her hand around Mr. Jiang's arm as they walk in slowly.

Andy whispers to Michael, also Fraser's church brother. "I told you they'd become one, didn't I?"

When they reach the altar, Mr. Jiang gently places his daughter's hand in Fraser's and says warmly, "I'm giving her to you, son. I know you will care for her for the rest of your life." Although he has called Fraser "son" before, this moment carries a much deeper significance for both of them.

As Mr. Jiang steps back, Kelsi lifts her eyes to Fraser. For a moment, the whole chapel seems to fade for both of them. Her smile is gentle, steady — the kind that has carried him through fear, doubt, and long nights of prayer. Up close, he can see the emotion shimmering in her eyes, and his breath catches without warning.

"You look... beautiful," he whispers, his voice cannot hide his joy.

Kelsi gives a small, shy nod, though her eyes are bright with joy.

"And you look nervous," she whispers back, her lips trembling with a smile.

Fraser laughs softly under his breath. "Only because this still feels like a miracle."

For a moment they simply stand there, hands clasped, hearts melting in the heartfelt wonder of what God has brought together.

At the reception, after a whirlwind of photos, drinks, and hors d'oeuvres, Kelsi spots Britney surrounded by a few young men trying to strike up conversation. But it is clear from her body language — arms crossed, smile tight — that she isn't really interested.

Kelsi walks over, gently hooks her arm through her sister's, and playfully pulls her away for more photos. The group of boys quickly disperses.

"Popular tonight, aren't you?" Kelsi teases." Seventeen and already breaking hearts."

Britney rolls her eyes. "They only see the Jiang name, not me." Britney's voice drops. "Sometimes I wish I could go somewhere and just be... nobody special."

She looks up at her sister, her voice sincere." I really admire you, sis. You know, Fritz got to know you — not the Jiang name — and he treats you no differently even after finding out."

With that, she steps away to greet Katie and Charlie, curious to learn more about the *Eyes of an Angel* they are wearing.

— ✦ —

Fraser and Kelsi finally settle into a quiet corner of the courtyard with Sarah, Jordan, Jalen, and Sabrina, ready to enjoy a relaxed conversation at last.

"I promise this honeymoon will be less dramatic than last time," Fraser tells Sabrina with a grin.

"You had a honeymoon before?" Jordan asks, genuinely puzzled — and clearly missing the joke.

"To a pair of lovers, every day is a honeymoon," Sarah jumps in, always ready with a quick save.

Everyone laughs.

111

Jalen adds, *"Eyes of an Angel* — what a fitting name. Seeing Katie and Charlie today… a blind child can see, a paralyzed one can move. I never knew my friend was such an angel." His admiration is unmistakable.

Before Fraser can respond, Sabrina chimes in, "Fraser, do you plan to put your invention into mass production?" She turns to Kelsi. "And does your dad agree to provide the funding?" It's clear she's wondering whether Jalen might one day have a stake in Fraser's research.

"I've spoken with my dad," Kelsi says. "He's planning to set up a charitable foundation for us to run. He'll provide the resources, and Fraser and I can use them however we see fit. He gets a tax write-off, and we get to serve those in need our way."

"It's a win-win," Jalen says with a satisfied sigh. "So what's your next research project, Fraser?"

"For you?" Fraser replies. "A pair of smart wedding rings. When you two start quarreling, just touch the rings together and you'll instantly know what your partner is thinking." He chuckles.

"Wow, that sounds amazing! When can we get them?" Jordan asks eagerly, glancing at Sarah.

"In twenty years," Fraser says with a laugh, earning giggles from everyone.

"Twenty years? That long?" Jordan frowns, clearly hoping for a miracle sooner.

"If you can last twenty years without them, you won't need them," Kelsi says, slipping her arm through Fraser's.

"We don't need smart rings." Her voice softens as she looks into his eyes. "We already read each other's minds."

Fraser holds her gaze, knowing she's right — love itself is the clearest signal.

For a moment, all of them simply sit there, letting peace settle around them like evening dew.

Sarah breaks the silence first. "You know," she says softly, "it's strange how everything worked out — the timing, the people, all of it. Almost like it was written that way."

Jordan nods, a quiet smile tugging at his lips. "Or engineered by Someone who knows what He's doing."

Sabrina leans against Jalen, her eyes following the last traces of sunlight across the courtyard. "We've all been waiting for this day — not just the wedding, but seeing how far grace can really go."

Jalen gives her hand a gentle squeeze, his gaze resting on Fraser. "Yeah," he says softly. "Everything he's built — *Eyes of an Angel*, the healings, all of it — started from love. Maybe that's how grace works… it just finds its way through people like him."

Their laughter is soft, their hearts at rest. No one says much after that. For once, silence feels like understanding — a quiet gratitude shared among friends who know that faith, like love, doesn't need a patent to last.

Fraser looks up at the evening sky as the sun slowly sets, painting the courtyard in shades of gold and rose.

Sensing his silence, Kelsi tilts her head toward him and smiles. "As I said, I can read your mind," she says softly. "You're frustrated — but what's bothering you?"

Fraser pulls her close and whispers, "You'll find out tonight."

Around them, their friends exchange knowing smiles — they don't need to know more.

That wedding night, as Kelsi lies in bed beside Fraser, she whispers, "Fritz, my dad handled all the wedding planning — but why have you still been so busy these past three months? Did you push back a project because of the wedding?"

Fraser pulls her close and smiles. "It only took me a week to program the algorithm that helped Patrick recover from his stroke... but it's taken me three months just to subscribe to a social media platform to promote *Eyes of an Angel* — and I'm still stuck."

He sighs, half amused, half resigned. "The posts stay stuck in draft mode, the 'Continue' button is always greyed out, and every time I try to get help, I just get a flood of spam emails."

Kelsi chuckles softly and loops her arms around his neck. "Maybe angels don't like using social media, Fritz. They follow by actions, not by tapping buttons."

For a moment, Fraser just looks at her, quietly moved. She says it like a playful tease, yet somehow it carries the calm wisdom of truth — the kind that reaches his heart before his mind can name it.

He exhales, smiling. "Then maybe I should just let grace go viral on its own. The world's never perfect…"

He turns toward her, brushing her hair back gently. "But tonight — it is."

Chapter 11 *A New Journey*

Princeton Meets Stanford

Five years after.

Britney presses her face against the airplane window, watching the East Coast disappear below. It is June, and she is finally heading to California.

Fresh out of Princeton with her molecular biology degree, she has been accepted to Stanford Medical School — a dream that feels surreal even now. Before the semester starts, she decides to take a trip to California to tour Stanford first, and to visit her sister and brother-in-law in Berkeley. It has been years since she has attended her sister's wedding, and she is thrilled to visit the Bay Area again.

It is early in the morning, and most of the passengers are dozing off. The cabin is very quiet.

"... I looked at the skies, running my hands over my eyes..."

Suddenly, Britney hears soft humming from the person next to her. Despite the low volume, her sharp hearing picks up the tune immediately. She loves oldies and immediately recognizes it as the Bee Gees' "I Started a Joke". Despite her privileged upbringing — or perhaps because of it — the melancholy in the lyrics touches something deep inside her.

"... Till I finally died, which starts the whole world living Oh, if I'd only seen that the joke is on me..."

As the humming continues, Britney is unexpectedly overwhelmed with a wave of sadness. She couldn't quite understand why, but the melancholic lyrics resonate deeply within her.

She turns around and glances at her neighbor. He is a young man who appears to be in his late twenties and dresses quite formally, wearing a white shirt with a tie. Though he wears glasses, she notices a tear glistening in each of his closed eyes.

Britney finds herself drawn to his sadness. What could make someone so young look so defeated?

She considers talking to him, but her upbringing and the fact that she is a young woman caution her against speaking to strangers.

The flight attendant arrives and places drinks on their tray tables. "The plane will be landing in San Francisco in one hour," she announces.

Britney picks up her coffee cup, taking a sip while glancing at her neighbor again. Almost at the same time, he opens his eyes, sits up straight, and picks up his cup. Their eyes meet briefly. Unsure whether it is her beauty that has caught his attention or just a need for conversation, he nods and says, "Hi."

Out of politeness and curiosity, Britney smiles and nods back.

"Sorry if my humming bothered you," he says, noticing her Princeton shirt. "Are you from Princeton? I graduated from University of Pennsylvania." It seems like he wants to carry on a conversation with Britney.

"Oh, we're both from Ivy League schools! I just finished at Princeton and will be starting at Stanford next semester. Are you just visiting California?" Britney seems eager to use this opportunity to get to know him better and discover why he hummed that tune.

He keeps silent for a moment. "Oh, this is a business trip. By the way, I am Dillon." He extends his hand.

"I'm Britney, nice to meet you." Britney extends her hand and gives a firm handshake.

Running out of things to say, Dillon pulls out his iPad but hesitates, unsure of what to do next. Noticing this, Britney breaks the ice. "You've been living on the East Coast for a while. Have you been to California before?" she asks with a smile.

"Actually, I grew up in California, but this is my first business trip," Dillon says, gazing out the window as if lost in thought. He becomes silent.

Britney notices there is a touch of sadness in his eyes. "California seems to hold a story for him," Britney thinks. "Is it linked to his sadness when he expressed that the joke is on him?" She can't help but wonder, so she isn't giving up the conversation.

"Business trip? I'm still a student heading to medical school. What kind of work do you do, Dillon?" She finds that using someone's name in conversation often gets a better response.

"Oh, I'm a lawyer," Dillon replies. "I'm working on a court case and need to gather evidence." He then falls silent again.

Understanding that lawyers can't discuss their work in detail, Britney decides not to press further.

"The plane will be landing in ten minutes. Please return to your seat and fasten your seatbelt," announces the flight attendant.

Her heart lifts at the thought of seeing Kelsi, Fraser, and the kids. She wonders what brilliant invention Fraser is working on now. The idea of being with her family again fills her with excitement. "It would be perfect if Daniel is as smart as Daddy, and Tiffany is as talented an artist as Mommy."

After the plane lands and taxis to the gate, Britney and Dillon step out quietly together. Dillon seems deep in thought, and Britney doesn't dare disturb him.

As they exit the gate, a young woman rushes to Dillon and embraces him. "How was your flight? Are you hungry?" she asks warmly.

Britney watches as the woman reaches for Dillon's hand, and the two of them walk away together. Dillon glances back and gives Britney a small nod.

Something feels off about their embrace — distant, almost formal. Two people can touch and still be far apart. But when Fraser hugs Kelsi, the whole room can feel the spark between them.

Britney shakes her head. Not her business.

When she reaches the curbside, Fraser is already waiting in front of his SUV. She quickly walks over and embraces her brother-in-law. Kelsi steps out of the SUV with open arms and says, "Hey Brit, you seem to grow taller every time I see you!"

Britney turns to her sister and gives her a big hug. "Where are the kids? Are they at home with the nanny?" she asks.

"Tiffany is sleeping in the car, and Daniel is at home with Rose," Kelsi replies. "Come on in, and we can catch up."

Britney settles into the SUV next to the sleeping three-year-old, while Fraser opens the trunk and begins loading the luggage.

As Fraser is driving, Kelsi turns to Britney and asks, "How are Mom, Dad, and Pat? I know you spent a few weeks in Hong Kong before coming here."

120

"They're all doing well," Britney replies with a smile. "The last time we saw Pat was at our family reunion two years ago. Back then he was still using crutches, but not anymore. He can walk on his own now, though he still has a slight limp. His speech is almost back to normal, too. Mom let him resume his duties as the restaurant manager last year."

"Meet anybody interesting at Princeton, Brit?" Kelsi asks. She knows Britney can handle the academics, but she's more curious about her sister's social life at such a nerdy university.

"Not really," Britney chuckles. "A lot of people tried to make friends with me, but I knew it was only because they knew I was from the Jiang family." She knows her looks attract plenty of attention too, but she can't say that in front of her sister.

Suddenly, her thoughts drift to Dillon. She's used to guys trying hard to talk to her — but Dillon stayed quiet, even when she made the effort. *He seemed to enjoy chatting with me at first...but whenever California came up, he shut down. Why?* She wonders.

Noticing her silence, Fraser glances at her through the rearview mirror. "Hey, Brit — thinking of your boyfriend?" he teases.

"No, not a boyfriend," Britney replies quickly. "Does your AI assistant think I'm thinking about a non-existent boyfriend? You need to modify your algorithm."

"Don't need AI to tell me," Fraser shoots back with a grin. "Your sister has that exact look whenever she thinks of me."

Kelsi gently punches his arm and giggles.

They arrive at their house in Berkeley Hills. Kelsi gets out of the car and carefully lifts the sleeping Tiffany onto her shoulder, while Fraser and Britney handle the luggage and head inside.

Britney rushes to the baby's crib and finds the nanny feeding little Daniel.

"Hi, Daniel, I'm your auntie Britney," she says, waving at the baby. Amazingly, Daniel raises his tiny hands, looks at his auntie with his big eyes, and smiles back.

Britney immediately picks him up into her arms and kisses him as he mumbles, "Arr-tee."

Kelsi steps in and says with a motherly smile, "He's fifteen months old now and just starting to learn how to talk." She gently places Tiffany in a bigger crib. "Let me show you to your room."

After dinner, the sisters relax in the lounge and chat.

"What is Fritz up to these days?" Britney asks curiously. "Sarah and Sabrina mentioned he worked on a pair of smart wedding rings that let partners read each other's minds. Is that for real?"

"That is his pet project, but he didn't actually spend a lot of time on it," Kelsi replies with a smile. "He spends a lot of time with the kids, even changing their diapers. I really didn't expect that from him. The rings didn't turn out completely successful. Sometimes you can catch bits and pieces of each other's thoughts, but never simultaneously."

"That's quite impressive enough. Oh, Sis, can you play the Bee Gee's 'I Started a Joke'?" Britney suddenly asks Kelsi, though she isn't sure why.

"Brit, that's a really old song. It's not a love song at all. Why do you want to hear it?" Kelsi is surprised by the request, thinking Britney would be more interested in love and romantic tunes given her age.

"Because I heard someone humming it during my flight here, and now I'm curious about what the song is about," Britney explains to her sister.

Kelsi steps toward the piano. "I've heard this tune a few times but never played it." She opens her iPad to find the sheet music.

As she starts playing, Fraser walks in. "A concert of oldies? Who picked this song?" He sits down with his coffee. "Or are we playing 'Name That Tune'? I Started a Joke sung by Robin Gibb of the Bee Gees in 1968." His knowledge of oldies is as impressive as his skills in computing and cooking.

"Oh Fritz, the guy sitting next to me on the flight was humming this tune. I noticed tears in his closed eyes. When we started talking, he went silent at the mention of California. He seemed pretty sad, even when he walked off with his girlfriend. He's a lawyer." Britney explains to Fraser in more detail than usual, perhaps seeking his insight as a man.

"Brit, he must have been quite good-looking for you to notice all that," Fraser teases his sister-in-law. "There aren't many sad lawyers I know. If a lawyer is sad, he must have lost a case he should have won." He pauses before adding, "So I guess he might have lost a case in California. But if he has a girlfriend, she'll take care of him. Definitely not you!" he added with a chuckle.

"Even if he's better looking than you, there's nothing more I can do because I don't have his contact number." Britney says, her outspoken nature contrasting with her sister's. Kelsi is just sitting on the piano bench smiling, enjoying their conversation.

The next day, Fraser has an online conference, and Kelsi stays home to take care of Daniel and Tiffany because Nanny Rose has the day off. Fraser let Britney use his SUV to drive to Stanford.

After the campus tour, Britney heads to the bookstore to pick up some textbooks. Carrying the books in a paper bag, she walks out, but the parking lot is far, and the books are heavy. She struggles for a few minutes before the paper bag rips open, spilling all the books onto the ground.

"Darn! I should have asked for double bags!" she mutters, bending down to pick up the scattered books. Just then, she hears a gentle voice with a distinguished English accent: "Please, let me help you." She looks up to see a man bending down a little further away, picking up her books.

The man walks toward her, holding a stack of books. He is in his late thirties, clean-cut with a groomed mustache.

"Thank you so much," Britney says, only then realizing her arms are completely full. She laughs, a little flustered. The man catches her glance and says warmly, "May I walk you to your car?"

With no better option, Britney agrees, and they head toward the parking lot together.

"Did you come for the campus tour today? Are you starting at Stanford this semester?" the man asks, breaking the ice. "By the way, I'm Colin. I work here — welcome to Stanford."

"I'm Britney, and I'll be starting my first year of medical school here. This campus is so beautiful!" Britney responds cheerfully.

"I'm glad you like it. You'll be spending at least four years here. Where did you graduate from, if you don't mind me asking?" Colin inquires politely.

"I'm from Princeton. The difference between the East Coast and the West is huge!" They chat as they approach the SUV.

As Britney opens the trunk and puts the books inside, Colin glances at the SUV and the license plates. "This isn't your car, is it? You're Kelsi's sister and Fraser's sister-in-law, right?"

"Oh, you recognize this car?" Britney asks, surprised. "Yes, it's Fraser's. You recognize his license plate number?"

"Not exactly," Colin explains. "But I recognize the Carnegie Mellon University Alumni license plate frame. Not many cars have that."

"You must be a good friend of his. We should all get together for lunch or coffee sometime," Britney suggests cheerfully.

Colin responds with a warm smile.

Chapter 12 *Faith and Responsibility*

Righteousness vs. Due Diligence

≈ ≈ ≈

After dinner, they relax in the lounge, chatting as usual.

"What kind of conference are you attending today, Fritz? You seem a bit distracted, and you've been coming down for coffee and snacks quite often," Kelsi asks with a smile.

Fraser takes a sip of his coffee before replying, "Someone has been making counterfeit versions of the *'Eyes of an Angel'*. A customer used one and got hurt. Now there's a lawsuit that's dragging our patented product into it. But honestly, I'm just a technical guy—I hardly know anything about legal matters. Mr. Liu from Dad's patent team is handling the case, so I've been pretty bored."

"That sounds complicated," Kelsi responds. "The knockoff is probably made outside the country, and we're being sued because they see us as the ones with deep pockets."

"Hey Brit, how is your day at Stanford? Settling in okay?" Fraser turns to her with a smile.

"The campus is gorgeous!" Britney replies, her eyes lighting up. "But I've heard the med school here is no joke. I just hope I can keep up."

Fraser chuckles softly. "I'm sure you will."

Kelsi leans in. "Medicine? I thought you are more into research, Brit."

"I am," Britney nods thoughtfully. "But after seeing what Fritz did for Pat, and how he helped Katie and Charlie... I realize healing people matters more to me than theories and data. I want to make that kind of difference." Her voice softens. "For me, the mind isn't enough—the heart has to lead too."

There is a short pause before she brightens again and shifts the subject.

"Oh! Fritz, do you know a guy named Colin? He works at Stanford. My paper bag tore up and all my books spilled everywhere. He helped me pick them up and even carried them to your car. Said he recognized your SUV."

"Really? He carried your books? Guess what—he's Dr. Stephens! The one who does the groundbreaking research on AI and brainwaves with me!" Fraser exclaimed, clearly excited. "He's the only person who's ever recognizes my Carnegie license frame. He's a Carnegie alumnus too, about eight years ahead of me."

"Wow, is he as smart as you? But he didn't seem like a typical nerd. He is a perfect gentleman," Britney is not shy to express her feelings.

Kelsi chimes in with a playful grin, "Does Fritz look like a nerd to you? I've met Dr. Stephens a few times, and it makes sense that they're good friends—they're cut from the same cloth." She glances at Fraser lovingly and smiles.

— ✦ —

The next morning, Britney wakes up later than usual. She has been staying up late chatting with her besties from Princeton, continuing well into the early morning on the East Coast.

When she finally comes downstairs, Kelsi is busy feeding Tiffany and Daniel.

"Did you sleep well last night, Brit? Breakfast is in the kitchen," Kelsi greets her warmly.

After having a light breakfast, Britney passes by the office and notices Fraser deep in conversation with two men. She immediately recognizes one of them as Mr. Liu, their patent lawyer. The other man has his back to the door, making it hard for her to see his face, but there is something familiar about his silhouette.

"Is that Dillon? What's he doing here with Mr. Liu?" Britney wonders, recalling the lawsuit Fraser has mentioned the night before. "Dillon's a lawyer —could he be involved in this case?" Her curiosity tells her to wait outside to find out more.

Finally, Britney sees Dillon shaking hands with Fraser and Mr. Liu before he heads out. She quickly steps out of sight, not wanting Dillon to know she is connected to the Jiang family — though she isn't entirely sure why she feels that way.

After Dillon leaves, Britney waits a bit longer until Mr. Liu also departs. She knows it wouldn't be polite to interrupt Fraser while he still has a guest in his office.

As soon as Fraser steps out of his office, Britney walks over, unable to contain her curiosity. "Hey, Fritz, is Mr. Liu here because of the lawsuit you mentioned last night?"

"Yes, Brit," Fraser replies with a sigh. "He came with the defendant's lawyer. Let's grab Kelsi, and I'll fill you in on the details."

They gather in the family room after Kelsi has sung the kids to sleep. Fraser begins with another heavy sigh. "Our *'Eyes of an Angel'* device is highly specialized and requires proper training and certification to use. It's crucial that users understand its limitations first."

He pauses briefly, then continues. "This product is only available to a select group of customers, along with detailed application information. It's not sold online. But somehow, Mr. Gonzalez, the plaintiff, managed to get his hands on it. He lives in Philadelphia, and his wife is legally blind. He wanted to use it to help her gain more independence."

He takes a sip of his coffee before going on. "But not long after she started using it, she was hit by a car in a hit-and-run accident. Now she's in a coma. This happened two months ago," he adds, his voice growing more serious.

"That's awful," Kelsi says as her eyes turn wet. "Does Mr. Gonzalez have children?" Being a mother, she is obviously concerned about this unfortunate family.

Fraser nods, his voice tinged with sadness. "Mrs. Gonzalez is in her early forties. They have two daughters, one twelve and the other nine."

"What's Dillon's role in the lawsuit?" Britney asks, her curiosity getting the better of her.

Fraser looks surprised. "Oh, you know Dillon? He's the defendant's lawyer. Is he the one who serenaded you on your flight?" he adds with a chuckle.

Britney smiles slightly. "Yes, that's him. Did they win the case? What exactly is Mr. Gonzalez suing for?"

"He's suing the company that sold him the *'Eyes of an Angel'* device for ten million dollars, and Dillon is their defense attorney," Fraser explains with a heavy sigh. "Mr. Gonzalez isn't well-educated and struggles with English. Dillon argued that the device is misused because the instructions weren't properly followed. As a result, the plaintiff lost the case, received nothing, and was ordered to pay the legal fees."

"Wait, you mentioned a knockoff' yesterday." Britney interrupts, her brow furrowing. "So Mr. Gonzalez isn't actually using our product? Why is Dillon here if we're not being sued? We have our own lawyers too."

Fraser's voice softens as he answers. "We had a long talk with Dillon this morning. It turns out they aren't suing us at all. Mr. Gonzalez is a taxi driver in Philadelphia, but with most people opting for Uber or Lyft these days, his income has been dwindling."

He sighs and continues. "He's trying to support his two daughters and cover the medical bills for his wife, who's in a coma. Dillon sees all of this and actually hopes he'd lose the lawsuit so that Mr. Gonzalez could get some compensation."

Fraser's voice cracks with emotion as tears well up in his eyes.

Kelsi hands him a tissue, her eyes full of sympathy, as Fraser continues. "During the lawsuit, Dillon and his tech-savvy colleagues thoroughly examined the '*Eyes of an Angel*' device and discovered it was likely a counterfeit, not our patented version. He reached out to me for more insights, hoping to prove that the company was illegally selling knockoffs. If successful, it might lead to compensation that could help Gonzalez's family."

"That explains why he looked so down and hummed that song," Britney says, nodding thoughtfully." It's very unusual for a lawyer to hope he loses a case. He really does have a heart." she reflects.

Kelsi then chimes in. "We do have detailed records of our customers that bought the product directly from us. It should be quite easy to trace it back to the seller, right?"

Fraser shakes his head slightly. "It's not that simple, Kelsi. Many of our customers are institutions like hospitals and rehab centers that purchase in bulk. They're not supposed to resell them to individual patients, but some units might end up on the secondary market."

"I really hope Dillon can pull this off. It's rare to find a lawyer with such integrity these days," Britney says with a touch of admiration. She isn't sure why, but suddenly Dillon seems different—steadier, kinder, worth paying attention to.

After lunch, while Britney is playing with Tiffany and Daniel, her phone rings.

"Hey, Britney! Are you free today? Want to go shopping together?" Chloe's voice comes through.

Britney brightens. "Hi, Chloe! I'd love to. Pick me up at two."

Chloe is one of Britney's besties from Princeton. They have been roommates for a year, though in different fields. Chloe's family lives in the Bay Area, and she is about to start her PhD in mathematics at UCLA.

The two girls have a fantastic time spending the afternoon shopping, chatting, and catching up on their campus lives. As dinner time approaches, they decide to stop by a Korean restaurant.

"Let's have Korean BBQ today," Chloe suggests. "The Korean food in Princeton is terrible, and this place has a long line, so it must be good."

They get a number and wait outside, chatting as their turn approaches. Just then, a couple walks by.

"Chloe Park! Are you in Princeton? I didn't expect to see you here!" The woman greets her, though with a hint of hostility in her voice.

"Cynthia Cho! You do realize it's summer, and I've already graduated, right?" Chloe retorts, matching the unfriendly vibe.

Britney, sensing the tension between them, glances at the couple for a better look.

"Dillon!" She exclaims. "Remember me, Britney? The one who sat next to you on the flight here?" She isn't sure why she feels excited to see Dillon again.

Dillon glances awkwardly between the three women, then gives Britney a silent nod.

Cynthia tugs on Dillon's arm. "This line is too long. Let's find somewhere else to eat." Without another word, they leave the restaurant.

Moments later, Britney and Chloe are led to their table and settle in.

"Who is this Cynthia? You two don't seem to get along," Britney couldn't help asking.

Chloe takes a sip of water before answering. "She's been my classmate since middle school. We are always the top two in our class, constantly competing with each other." She sighs. "It isn't just about academics, it is everything." Then, with a

134

curious glance, she added, "So, you know Dillon? I notice you talk to him."

"I don't really know him, Chloe," Britney recalls Dillon's look when he saw Chloe, so she chose her words carefully." He sat next to me on the flight here, so we chatted a bit. We didn't even exchange numbers." Her instincts tell her there is more to the story between Dillon, Chloe, and Cynthia.

Chloe doesn't hold back with her best friend. "Dillon was actually my boyfriend back in eleventh grade. Cynthia and I met him at a party at UC Davis, where he was a student," she confesses. "He chose me first, and we dated for two years. But then Cynthia swooped in. She's incredibly aggressive and will do anything to get what she wants."

"She took Dillon away from you?" Britney exclaims. "Come on — no one can make a guy do that. He chose her? Seriously? You're way prettier than she is!"

"Dillon's a good guy, but he's weak," Chloe says bluntly. "Cynthia offered him things I wouldn't. You know what I mean?" She sighs, clearly still affected by the memory.

Britney immediately caught her meaning. She decides not to press further, but after a pause, she can't help herself. "How can someone so wishy-washy be a lawyer?" Britney asks.

Chloe looks surprised. "He's a lawyer? I didn't know that. Did he tell you on the plane? Of course, you're the Queen of our graduation class — you always get people to open up!" She teases her best friend.

Britney laughs, "It's only because you all wear glasses and I don't," she picks up the sense of humor from her brother-in-law.

The waiter arrives to set up the BBQ grill and places the sliced meats on the table.

"Let's eat and not talk about them." Chloe says as she picks up her chopsticks.

— ✦ —

Later that night, after a shower, Britney lies in bed, her thoughts drifting.

"So Dillon's a local from the Bay Area, and Chloe and Cynthia are part of his California story. And he was humming 'the joke is on him'... Is he regretting choosing Cynthia now?" The pieces start to fall into place.

"Why am I even thinking about him? He's tangled up with two women, and one of them is my best friend. I should know better." She turns, pulling the blanket up as if it could shut him out.

Instead, Dillon lingers — tear-streaked, humming softly, unaware of her watching. She doesn't even realize it's beginning—first curiosity, then admiration, then something warmer slipping in before she can stop it.

She gets out of bed and heads to the kitchen for a glass of milk, hoping it would help her sleep. As she passes the office, she notices Fraser still working at his computer. Deciding to chat with her brother-in-law, she steps inside.

"Still at it, Fritz?" she starts.

Fraser looks up from the monitor, smiling. "Hey, Brit. We missed you at dinner, so you must've had a good time with your friend. How is your day?" He leans back in his chair and sets his glasses down on the table, giving her his full attention.

Britney pulls up a chair and sits down. "We had a great time today. Guess who Chloe and I ran into—Dillon and his girlfriend!" she says, diving straight into the topic.

"Dillon? Attorney Dillon?" Fraser responds with a grin. "Did you talk to him? How much did he charge you?" As always, he couldn't resist teasing his sister-in-law.

"Not sure yet—he might send you the bill later," Britney says with a quick grin.

"Actually, he was Chloe's boyfriend before, and now he's with Cynthia. Chloe and Cynthia were high school classmates, so it was a bit awkward when we all met."

She pauses, suddenly aware of her own heartbeat for reasons she can't explain.

"Um… do you ever like any other girl besides my sister? And how do you choose between them?" Her tone stays even, almost teasing, but the question feels oddly personal—and she isn't sure why she cares so much about the answer.

Fraser smiles warmly. "Yes, it's no secret, and your sister knows all about it. Six months after I met and fell for her, another girl entered our lives. Sarah is warm and kind-hearted,

137

always willing to serve others. She is like an angel to me." As he says this, Britney can sense the love and admiration in his voice.

"That's Sarah? I remember meeting her and Jordan at your wedding. She's so beautiful and graceful! No wonder you fell for her," she says, eager to hear more.

Fraser smiles softly. "I prayed to God, wondering why Sarah had come into my life. Then it hit me—God sent her with a message. She let me know about Katie and Charlie. I needed to use my talents to help those in need. That's how I came to invent *'Eyes of an Angel'*, and your sister made it possible to bring them to the world. She's my true angel."

His eyes glisten as he adds softly, "But Sarah... she's still an angel to me. We're still very good friends."

He pauses, gathering his thoughts. "Everyone's story is unique. When I was talking with Dillon, I could tell how meticulous he was—always covering every detail to secure the outcome he wanted. That's what a lawyer does."

Fraser lets out a small breath. "But love and emotions don't work that way. You can't plan them, and you definitely can't predict how things will turn out." His mind flickers to that church performance six years ago, the one that changed everything.

"All we can do is give our best. And the rest..." He glances out the window, voice turning gentle. "God will program that part for us."

Britney forces a tiny smirk. "Okay, I get it. Follow my heart. Just don't start charging me for life advice, Fritz."

"But what are you working on? It's pretty late." She adds.

Fraser's voice softens as he responds, "When Dillon told me this morning that Mrs. Gonzalez was in a coma after the accident, I was really moved and wanted to do something. It felt like a calling, just like when I felt driven to help Katie, Charlie, and Pat."

He gives a sigh. "But with a coma patient, there's no active brainwave or vision. Feeding the patient data seems pointless." He pauses briefly. "I've been thinking about it all afternoon. I'm heading to Philadelphia in a few days to visit the Gonzalez family. Maybe being there will spark some new ideas."

"Oh, Fritz, you're so kind. No wonder my sister loves you so much." Britney steps forward, giving Fraser a warm hug. "Good night," she whispers.

Chapter 13 *Exchanges Over Coffee*

Questions of the Heart

Britney and Chloe are sitting in a Starbucks chatting over coffee.

"So, Dillon actually came by my sister's place yesterday," Britney begins, her tone casual but intriguing. "He needed to talk to my brother-in-law about a lawsuit he's working on."

Chloe's eyes widen in surprise. "Your brother-in-law? Isn't he the guy who invented those *'Eyes of an Angel'* goggles that help blind people see?" she asks, clearly taken aback. "Wait, is Dillon suing him?"

"No, we're not involved in the lawsuit," Britney explains, beginning to fill Chloe in on what she knows about the case.

"So, Dillon is trying to get compensation from the company selling counterfeits? Could that be Kyle's company?" Chloe speaks out her thoughts. "Kyle is Cynthia's brother. He tried to date me before I left for Princeton, but I never liked him. He is running a shady business, selling counterfeits online under a fake company name. I've never had much respect for people like that."

"Oh, that makes sense now. If he gets sued, it's only natural he'd turn to his sister's attorney boyfriend for defense, keeping it all in the family." Britney remarks. "So it's no surprise Dillon won the case quickly for them. But now he's suing them again for compensation? That's getting pretty messy."

"Yes, I do feel sorry for him," Chloe says with a sigh.

"Chloe, do you still have feelings for him? If he left Cynthia and wanted to come back to you, would you take him back?" Britney suddenly asks, the question seeming as much for herself as for Chloe.

"Honestly, probably not," Chloe replies quietly. "He actually reached out to me two years ago, saying he is breaking up with Cynthia and wanted to see me. Philadelphia isn't far from Princeton, after all." She pauses for a moment. "But I turned him down. It's hard to rebuild something with someone once the trust is gone."

"Doesn't seem like he's actually broken up with Cynthia," Britney comments.

"Exactly," Chloe nods. "He's the type who always keeps an escape route. That's what I don't like about him. For me, love isn't about having a backup plan. You're either in it or you're

141

not. If it falls apart, you pick up the pieces, stand tall, and move forward." She shares her thoughts on love with her best friend.

When Britney returns home, she sees Fraser and Kelsi walking out with a guest.

"Colin! What brings you here?" she asks, immediately walking over to greet him.

"I came to see you, but since you weren't home, I had to settle for chatting with Kelsi and Fraser," Colin replies with a warm smile.

Not sure if Colin is being serious or joking, Britney playfully responds, "You must've come for Fritz's banana bread and mochi cakes. I came all the way from Princeton to try them too!"

"Oh, then I probably shouldn't have brought Mrs. Fields cookies," Colin laughs. "Anyway, I've got to run. See you later at Stanford."

Fraser and Kelsi stand by the door, smiling at each other.

Once they are all back inside, Britney looks as if she is about to ask something, but Fraser speaks first.

"I invited Colin over to discuss the symptoms and bodily functions of coma patients. He's an expert in human physiology," Fraser explains, pausing with a grin. "And, by the way, he did ask about you once we are done."

"Did he give you any new ideas for your research? So, are you headed to Philadelphia soon?" Britney replies, deliberately ignoring the last part of what he says.

"Yes, in three days. But I have to contact Dillon for more information about the Gonzalez family first before I go."

They step into the lounge, where Kelsi immediately turns her attention to Tiffany and Daniel, while Rose goes to the kitchen to prepare dinner.

Fraser and Britney sit down across the coffee table from each other. Fraser leans in, eyes brightening.

"Colin actually gave me some inspiration," he says. "Even if a coma patient has lost certain brain functions, or vision, or the ability to respond… hearing is often the last sense to go."

He pauses, letting the thought land. "And we forget this sometimes, but a coma patient is still alive — breathing, warm, with a beating heart."

His voice rises with excitement. "If they can still hear, then part of them might still be searching for a way back."

"Breathing and heartbeat? How could that help someone wake up?" Britney asks, still puzzled by her brother-in-law's line of thought.

"I don't know yet," Fraser admits, his gaze shifting to the cross on the wall. " But our Lord does," he whispers softly.

After a moment of silence, Britney speaks up, "Hey Fritz, I had coffee with Chloe today, and she told me more about Dillon. It turns out that the company that sold the counterfeit to Mr. Gonzalez might be run by Cynthia's brother." With her sister busy with the kids, she really needs someone to talk to.

"Cynthia? Is that his current girlfriend? So, he won a case for her family and now wants to sue them back?" Fraser chuckles. "Brit, if I were you, I'd steer clear and not get involved. But then again, I'm not you—and I'm not a girl in love."

Britney's cheeks flush slightly. She isn't sure why she keeps bringing up Dillon. Maybe it is because she senses he is unhappy with Cynthia, and Chloe doesn't seem to want him back. She forgets that Dillon barely knows her—just her name, really.

Fraser notices her sudden quietness and the slight blush on her face, and realizes his hunch is right. He knows love could take hold without rhyme or reason.

"I get it," he says softly, handing her a cup of coffee. "But it's important to learn more about him first. I'll invite him to lunch tomorrow, and you can just happen to stop by." He gently pats her shoulder. "Meeting here at home might not be ideal."

"Thanks, Fritz," Britney replies, grateful for his thoughtfulness. "Should I pretend to be someone else? Guys seem to treat me differently when they find out I'm from the Jiang family."

"Just be yourself," Fraser advises. "When you're true to who you are, that's when you really shine."

144

The next day at noon, Fraser meets Dillon at a quaint French bistro, tucks away from the nearby shopping mall.

After placing their orders, Fraser leans in and asks, "How long has Mrs. Gonzalez been in a coma?"

"About ten weeks," Dillon replies, handing a folder of documents to Fraser. "These are her medical records. Mr. Gonzalez gave his permission for you to have them. He's heard about you and is thrilled that you're willing to help his wife."

Fraser takes the folder and carefully slips it into his portfolio. "I'm not sure I can really help. A coma patient is so different from a handicapped patient, but I'll give it my best shot."

As he looks up, Fraser spots Kelsi and Britney walking into the bistro. He waves at the sisters. As they approach, Dillon stares at Britney and looks totally surprised. Britney glances at Dillon but decides to keep quiet.

Fraser stands to greet them, pulling out chairs for the sisters. "Dillon, this is my wife, Kelsi, and her sister, Britney," he says, introducing them with a warm smile. "Girls, this is Dillon, the attorney I've been telling you about who's working on Mr. Gonzalez's case."

As Britney sits down, she notices Dillon seems to want to say something but hesitates. *He recognizes me from when I was with Chloe and met Cynthia. Why is he so unsure of what to say? What kind of attorney is this?* She wonders, not realizing that even the best attorneys could find themselves in awkward situations.

145

Noticing the expressions on both Britney's and Dillon's faces, Kelsi smiles and asks, "Have you two met before?"

Britney quickly responds, "We met on my flight here and chatted a bit."

Dillon, uncertain how to proceed, adds," I didn't realize you are Mr. Lin's sister-in-law!"

Here we go again! Britney thinks, a bit disappointed. *Why does my family always have to come up in a conversation?*

After placing their orders, the four of them engage in casual conversation. Dillon occasionally glances at Britney but hesitates to address her directly. Normally at ease in social settings, Britney finds the unspoken tension between them increasingly uncomfortable.

As lunch finally comes to an end and they step out of the bistro, Dillon suddenly turns to Britney and asks, "Britney, would you like to grab a cup of coffee?"

Caught off guard by his request, especially after the awkwardness during lunch, Britney hesitates. The question is light. But she lets the pause stretch, caught between a quick yes and a polite no. The silence she creates carries more weight than the words themselves.

"Sure," she finally replies with a pleasant smile. "But you'll have to take me home afterward. You know where I live."

Fraser and Kelsi exchange amused glances.

— ✦ —

Inside Philz Coffee, they sit down, and a shared smile breaks the initial silence.

"Chloe must have told you about us. You two seem to be good friends," Dillon begins.

Britney nods. "She mentioned you three, but I only got her side of the story," she says thoughtfully.

"Remember we chatted on the plane? I found you really easy to talk to, but I have so much on my mind that I couldn't focus," Dillon admitted, finally opening up.

Not entirely sure if he is being sincere or just trying out a pickup line, Britney responds with a hint of humor, "I'm from Princeton, so I naturally analyze people. You seemed really troubled, and I couldn't help but wonder why." Actually, she is speaking the truth.

"Mr. Lin probably mentioned my case against Mr. Gonzalez," Dillon says with a little emotion. "He's suing my good friend Kyle—Cynthia's brother—for ten million dollars."

He pauses, then continues. "Initially, I had no clue that Kyle was dealing in counterfeits. I truly believed he was selling a legitimate patented product from Jiang Industries. But when Mr. Gonzalez filed the lawsuit, I realized it would pit us against a powerful company — a battle we'd likely lose. So, I took the easier route and denied the claim."

He sighs deeply. "But I haven't slept well ever since, especially thinking about poor Mrs. Gonzalez. Then it hit me — they weren't selling legitimate products, and now I feel compelled to take action."

"Why are you telling me all this? I'm not a law student, and I don't know much about legal matters," Britney responds with a hint of curiosity. "But I heard you're now seeking compensation from the seller's team. I know it must be tough to sue your girlfriend's family, and I wish you the best of luck."

"Thanks for listening. Chloe doesn't speak to me anymore, and Cynthia hates seeing me talk to other girls. That day, seeing you with Chloe while Cynthia is right there really threw me off."

He looks into Britney's eyes. "You're very approachable... and I'm really glad I have this chance to chat with you. Mr. Lin is a very kind and talented person. You are very lucky to have him as your brother-in-law."

Britney opens her mouth, then closes it again, caught off guard. "Well... I try," she says lightly, though a bright flutter tugs at her chest.

Dillon notices the quiet joy in her eyes, and a soft feeling settles over him too.

That evening at the dining table, Fraser and Kelsi keep smiling at Britney but say nothing. They'd love to hear what Dillon told her, but they know she needs time to think.

After dinner, Britney notices Fraser heading to his office, giving her a chance to chat with her sister alone.

"Did you have a good time talking with Dillon?" Kelsi asks warmly.

"Yeah, he just needed someone to talk to about his court case with his girlfriend's family. His ex-girlfriend is Chloe, and she's not speaking to him anymore," Britney replies briefly. Then, with curiosity, she adds," Why is Fritz going to his office now? He knows this is supposed to be family time!"

"Oh, he had a spark of inspiration about why loved ones can sometimes help coma patients more effectively than anyone else," Kelsi explains, searching for the right words. "This afternoon, we all recorded and digitized our heartbeats— mine, Tiffany's, Daniel's, Rose's, and his own. He must have found some kind of connection."

A small crease forms between Britney's brows. As a science major, she knows heartbeats are just electrical signals, patterns on a graph. But hearing Kelsi speak... she starts to see what Fraser is really chasing.

Not data.

Not logic.

But a kind of faith that lets him try things no one else would even bother attempting — things that look meaningless on the surface, yet somehow end up changing lives.

For the first time, Britney feels the faint pull of that belief, too.

Watching her sister, Kelsi adds, "Whenever he gets inspired like this, he's on the verge of working miracles. We don't know how—but we've seen it. The grace from above is real." Her voice is full of love and admiration.

The next morning, Britney drives Fraser to the airport. He is heading to Philadelphia to visit the Gonzalez family, while Kelsi stays home to watch the kids.

As they reach the gate, Fraser turns to Britney with a smile. "I'll be gone for about a week," he says. "I might be too busy to call every day, but I'll stay in touch with Colin. He's up to speed on what I'm working on." He pauses, giving her a playful look. "You should give him a call sometime. He enjoys talking with you."

With a grin, he adds, "Wait for my good news!" Then, with a final smile, he steps through the gate.

Chapter 14 *Prayer in the Night*

Emotion Reaches for Guidance

ৰ্গ ৰ্গ ৰ্গ

When Britney arrives home, she overhears Kelsi speaking on the phone.

"...he just left for a flight to Philadelphia. I'll pass along the good news. Thank you, Mr. Liu." Kelsi hangs up just as Britney walks in.

"Hey, Brit!" Kelsi greets her with a cheerful voice. "That is Mr. Liu. He says they discovered the *'Eyes of an Angel'* counterfeit is being produced in China, and they've identified the connection here in the States."

"Oh, really? What's our next move? Are we going to sue them?" Britney asks, her thoughts flashing to Dillon's situation with Cynthia's brother, Kyle.

"Not sure," Kelsi says. "Mr. Liu mentioned he'll reach out to Dillon to join forces in taking down the counterfeit company. Fritz must be relieved to hear that."

Britney returns to her room, lying on her bed, lost in thought.

"Did Dillon take me out for coffee because he wanted to talk to a therapist? Or is he actually interested in me?" she wonders.

Her thoughts begin to drift. She knows her looks often attracted attention from guys trying to socialize with her, but Dillon feels different. As a lawyer, he is skilled at talking to anyone about anything, yet he seemed shy and hesitant around her.

She is starting to realize that this might be how someone behaves when they have feelings for another person.

Then she thinks of Chloe and Cynthia. She shakes her head and buries it in her pillow. She prays the answer will find her heart before she has to choose.

Later that afternoon, Dillon calls.

"Hey, Britney, want to come out for a drink? I can pick you up in an hour if that works for you," he asks, this time with confidence.

An hour later, they are seated at Roundtable, chatting over pizza and beer.

"I spoke with Kyle about compensating Mr. Gonzalez, and he's not thrilled about it," Dillon says, getting straight to the point.

"I think that's the right move, Dillon. You approach him first, and if it can be settled out of court, that's even better," Britney

152

replies, sharing her thoughts. "But how did Kyle take it? Is there any room for negotiation?" she asks, raising a crucial question.

"He's furious. He's never been the calm type, Britney," Dillon recalls. "I'm not even asking for the ten million Mr. Gonzalez demanded—just a hundred thousand, which I know his business can cover. But he claimed it wasn't his problem and told me to back off. We've been friends for so long, but..." Dillon sighs.

"So, what's your next move? You're not giving up, are you?" Britney asks, her tone encouraging.

Touched by her concern, Dillon replies, "Your family's lawyer contacted me. With Jiang Industries backing the case, we might actually have a shot."

"Britney, are you free to catch a show this Wednesday? I'm thinking of seeing *Frozen*. I haven't been to a show in years, and I've heard it's really good." Suddenly, he shifts the conversation to asking for a date.

Britney is caught off guard but pleasantly surprised. Her heart starts pounding, but she has been through this kind of situation before.

She hesitates for a moment. "I'd love to, but that day is my nephew Daniel's birthday. I need to check with my sister about our plans. Since Fraser's not home, we'll probably have an online celebration." In reality, she doesn't even know when Daniel's birthday is.

Sensing this is a subtle rejection, Dillon could only reply, "Sure, you let me know."

— ✦ —

Later that night, alone in her room, Britney debates whether she should talk to Chloe or not.

Chloe still hasn't dated anyone seriously since Dillon. *That has to mean something, right?* Britney ponders. *Dillon says they don't talk anymore. But does that mean I'm supposed to take her place? Should I even want to?* She questions herself, with no clear answers in sight.

She picks up her phone.

— ✦ —

The next morning, as Britney comes down for breakfast, she is surprised to see Kelsi in the office, chatting with Dr. Stephens.

"Dr. Stephens, good morning! Fritz is in Philadelphia right now. What brings you here?" she asks, recalling that he must have known Fraser is out of town. She also remembers Fraser's hint.

"Good morning, Britney. Please, call me Colin. That's what you called me when we first met," Dr. Stephens replies, his tone as polite as ever. With a grin, he adds, "Since Fraser isn't here, I brought Mrs. Fields cookies for us to share." He hands her a bag of cookies, a small reminder of their previous encounter.

Britney chuckles, but Colin quickly shifts to a more serious tone. "I had a long conversation with Fraser this morning. He's exploring the idea that a coma patient might still be able to sense taste and smell. He's working on a way to tap into the patient's brain to find out."

"What? Tapping into a patient's brain?" Britney is completely perplexed. It sounds like science is pushing its own limits.

Kelsi jumps in, "Remember the smart wedding rings Fritz mentioned during our wedding? He made a prototype before Tiffany was born. We talk about it, remember?"

"But you told me it wasn't working well because the reading of thoughts is only one-way... Oh, a coma patient can't exchange thoughts!" Britney, being a science major, quickly understands what Fraser is getting at.

"Exactly!" Colin nods with approval. "Fraser asks me to review his design of the rings and see if there's potential to improve them. That's why I'm here—to borrow the rings and his notes."

"Colin, what you and Fraser are working on is beyond anything I can comprehend," Britney says with a smile as she opens the bag and pulls out a cookie.

Kelsi hands a portfolio to Colin. "Here are the data files, notes, and the rings. Fraser is incredibly meticulous. Fortunately, he's made two pairs. He has the revised version. This is the original pair."

Colin accepts the portfolio and turns to Britney. "Britney, would you like to join me for lunch?"

Britney hesitates, glancing at her sister.

Kelsi smiles warmly. "Go ahead, Brit. It's a great chance to get to know Colin better — you'll learn a lot."

— ✦ —

Back in Dillon's apartment, Cynthia is throwing a tantrum, her voice escalating to a shout. "Why are you asking Kyle to compensate Gonzalez when he lost the case? A hundred thousand dollars? Are you out of your mind?"

Dillon remains unshaken. "It's the least he can do. We thoroughly examined Mr. Gonzalez's helmet and goggles. Critical firmware components are missing, making them extremely dangerous to use without supervision."

He pauses, letting his words sink in before continuing, "If Mr. Gonzalez had been using genuine Jiang equipment, the accident might never have happened. In a significant way, your brother is responsible."

Before Cynthia could respond, Dillon continues. "Cynthia, this is between Kyle and me. You should stay out of it." His voice softens as he adds, "Let's go out for lunch."

They arrive at the same Korean restaurant where they had run into Chloe and Britney a couple of days earlier. As they walk in, Dillon immediately spots Britney in a corner, laughing and chatting with a British man over a sizzling barbecue grill.

Noticing that Britney might not see him, Dillon would normally step away. But this time, he walks up to her table, holding Cynthia's hand. "Hi, Britney, nice to see you here again," he says, surprised by his own newfound courage.

Britney looks up, smiling. "Oh, hi, Dillon! What a coincidence! And you must be... Cynthia? I'm Britney." Realizing she hasn't been formally introduced, she stands up and extends her hand.

Cynthia, noticing Chloe isn't present, hesitates before briefly shaking Britney's hand. "Hi," she responds, her tone somewhat restrained.

Britney quickly introduces everyone. "This is Dr. Stephens, and this is Dillon and Cynthia. Dr. Stephens works at Stanford and is a friend of my family. Enjoy your lunch!" she adds as she sits back down.

Uncertain how to proceed, Dillon and Cynthia walk to another corner of the restaurant and take their seats.

"Disappointed that Chloe isn't here? Looks like you'll have to settle for her friend today," Cynthia teases Dillon with a playful grin.

"I've already told you, Chloe and I are done. Why do you keep bringing it up? Let's just order." Dillon replies, his tone a bit sharper than usual.

At Britney's table, Colin notices that she has suddenly grown quiet.

"Is Dillon a close friend of yours?" he asks gently, sensing something is on her mind.

"No, he's just a casual acquaintance," Britney replies quietly. "I didn't really expect to see him here."

Colin's eyes twinkle with amusement. "Funny how you picked the same restaurant where you met him before. With so many restaurants around, it's a bit of a coincidence that he chose this one, too. Seems like he might have hoped to bump into you." He chuckles lightly.

Impressed by Colin's observations, Britney replies, "He's just a friend, and he's with his girlfriend Cynthia." She hesitates, suddenly unsure how much she should say—or how Colin might take it.

Colin simply nods, respecting her privacy and choosing not to press her further. They share a quiet moment, savoring their barbecue.

Britney breaks the silence, her curiosity piques. "Colin, do you think it's possible to tap into a coma patient's brain?"

Colin considers her question seriously. "Yes and no, Britney. With our current technology, we're not quite there yet," he replies thoughtfully. "But when it comes to your brother-in-law, it might be different. He has something many of us lack— faith. As a Catholic, I believe humans have their limitations, but Fraser's faith often pushes beyond those boundaries."

Noticing the admiration in Britney's eyes, Colin continues, "He once told me that when he designed the smart wedding rings years ago, he felt guided by God to make them one-way instead of two-way. He believed there was a purpose behind that choice — something meant for this moment, to help a coma patient. That kind of faith is remarkable. I'm sure he'll make a difference in Philadelphia."

Britney lowers her gaze, quietly moved. There's a steadiness in Fraser's faith that stirs something she didn't realize she'd been missing — the kind of certainty that makes others believe, even when they don't fully understand it.

— ✦ —

That evening, when Britney arrives home, Kelsi greets her with a warm smile.

"How is your lunch with Dr. Stephens?" she asks eagerly, barely waiting for Britney to reach the living room.

"It is a good lunch. We had a great conversation—he's such a knowledgeable gentleman," Britney replies with a smile. "But then Dillon and his girlfriend showed up. It got a little awkward." Britney adds, subtly hinting that she might need some advice.

Kelsi pauses for a moment. "How did Dillon react when he saw you and Colin?" She uses Dr. Stephens' first name to make it feel more personal.

"He just walked by and said hi. After I introduced Colin, Cynthia quickly pulled him away."

"Did that surprise you?" Kelsi asks thoughtfully. "He saw you with another man while he is with someone else. What more could he have done?"

Britney is speechless. She steps into the lounge and starts playing with the kids.

Kelsi follows in her footsteps into the lounge.

"I know what you're thinking. I'm your sister, Brit," she says warmly with a smile. "You are hoping Dillon would show some jealousy when he saw Colin, but you forgot he is with another woman." Kelsi says it gently, as if reading Britney's thoughts before she can hide them.

Britney gently lays Tiffany down in her crib, then turns to her sister. "Yes, I was jealous when I saw him holding hands with Cynthia," she admits, tears rolling down her cheeks. "I've only known him for a few days, but I can't stop thinking about him... I was enjoying my time with Colin until he showed up."

Kelsi approaches and wraps her arm around Britney's shoulder. "I totally understand how you feel, Brit," she says softly, her mind drifting back to the moment when Fraser called Sarah onto the stage five years ago. "Emotions can surface without any clear reason. Sometimes our hearts move faster than our minds can make sense of."

Britney nods, though she doesn't quite know why her chest feels so heavy. It isn't love — not yet — but something in Dillon's voice, the way he carries himself, has lingered longer than she expected. Maybe it's admiration. Maybe it's curiosity. Or maybe it's just the echo of something she's been waiting to feel.

"What should I do, Sis?" she asks, her voice trembling with tears.

"You need to figure out how he really feels about you," Kelsi advises gently. "It's complicated—especially since he first knew Chloe and now has Cynthia. But you have to find out."

160

She pulls Britney into a warm embrace, letting her dry out her tears.

Suddenly, Kelsi asks softly, "Brit, what do you think of Colin? It seems like he's quite fond of you."

Caught off guard by her sister's question, Britney replies, "I'm not sure. He's a really nice guy, but I barely know him. He's definitely as smart as Fritz. Does he have a family?" she finally asks.

Kelsi hesitates before answering, "I only know he was divorced two years ago after seven years of marriage," she says. "According to Fritz, he was so devoted to his research that he neglected his wife. They had one son, and he let his wife take custody." Though Kelsi doesn't like bringing this up, she feels it is important for her sister to know.

Britney just nods. "I had a feeling that might be the case. He's too nice to have never been married at his age," she says, regaining her composure. "But he's almost twenty years older than me. Why would he be interested in me?" Though, deep down, she knows that many men are often attracted to much younger women.

That night, Britney lies in bed, unable to sleep. Images of Dillon and Colin keep flashing through her mind.

Then she remembers what Fraser has told her about his choice between Kelsi and Sarah. Feeling inspired, she gets up, kneels beside her bed, and buries her face in her hands. She doesn't pray often, being more of a Sunday morning Christian, but in that moment, she feels the need to talk to her Lord.

Chapter 15 *Justice and Integrity*

Love's Power to Change

The next morning, while the sisters are having breakfast, Britney's phone rings. She answers it quickly, her heart skipping a beat.

"Hey, Britney! Are you free today? Want to hang out today? My family has an event, and I'm feeling a bit bored." Chloe's voice comes through.

Britney, a little let down that it isn't Dillon, replies, "Sure, pick me up in an hour." She just wants to get out of the house.

"Is that Chloe?" Kelsi asks softly. "This might be a good opportunity to learn more about her relationship with Dillon, but please be subtle," she advises.

Just after Britney left the house, Kelsi's phone rings. It is Mr. Liu.

"Kelsi, we're proceeding with a lawsuit against the company that sold Mr. Gonzalez the counterfeit *'Eyes of an Angel'* product. Dillon will be our plaintiff attorney, with support from our patent team. The trial is scheduled for four days from now, just in time for Fraser's return. He might be called in as an expert witness," Mr. Liu explains.

"That's fantastic news! Fraser will be back the day after tomorrow. He'll be thrilled to know this could help the Gonzalez family," Kelsi responds, her excitement clear in her voice.

Meanwhile, Britney and Chloe stroll through the mall. Chloe notices that Britney is unusually quiet—not her ever-cheerful self—and suggests they find a bar, sit down, and talk over a beer.

Once they settle in, Britney starts pouring her heart out—how torn she feels between Colin's gentle kindness and Dillon's magnetic pull.

Chloe leans forward and sets her glass down with a quiet clink. "Brit, you can't string them along," she says, her voice gentle but edged with steel. "Colin deserves honesty, and Dillon deserves clarity. What do you really want?" It isn't judgment— just love spoken firmly.

Britney flushes with irritation. *I just want someone to listen. Why can't she let me figure this out myself?* She looks away from Chloe's steady gaze.

But the sting fades as quickly as it came, replaced by something else—gratitude. Chloe sees the truth she hasn't dared admit and loves her enough to say it out loud.

She swirls what's left of her beer, her mind finally realizing she can't hide from her own feelings forever.

— ✦ —

Meanwhile, in Philadelphia, Fraser sits alone in Denny's restaurant, quietly eating lunch while deep in thought.

"Her heart responded to the children's presence but barely reacted to Carlos. Almost like she didn't recognize him as family. That's odd," Fraser muses, lost in thought.

"He mentioned this is her second marriage and that the first daughter wasn't his. Could her heart still be connected to her first husband, not Carlos?" Fraser wonders, delving into Mrs. Gonzalez's personal life. "Maybe if I could locate Lucia's first husband... but Carlos says he'd been dead for a while."

Fraser sighs, realizing he's reached a dead end.

That evening, he returns to the hospital to check on Lucia. He knows that when doors won't open, prayer often looks for windows.

As he steps into her room, he finds Carlos and his two daughters gathered around her bed, their faces streaked with tears. They whisper softly in Spanish—words he can't fully understand, though their grief needs no translation.

When they notice him, Carlos looks up.

165

"Thank you for everything you've done, Mr. Fraser," he says gratefully. "We know you tried your best. We understand you're not God." He gives a small nod, then gently ushers the children out.

Fraser moves closer to Lucia's bedside. Her face is still damp from their tears. He picks up a towel and begins wiping them away—when a faint movement flutters through her cheek.

A spark rises in him, quick and urgent.

He reaches for the smart wedding rings and connects them to his laptop. Then he bows his head, whispering a silent prayer, pouring every longing he has into this fragile moment.

The monitor flickers with a faint rhythm—fragile, but real.

Fraser closes his eyes, letting the pulse wash through him: hopeful, graceful, alive. What the mind couldn't reach, a rhythm might.

And he believes love is the only rhythm strong enough to cross the silence.

Back in the Bay Area, Dillon is preparing his case against Kyle, knowing full well the consequences it might bring. Cynthia's going to be furious, and this could very well be the end of our relationship. *But do I even want it to continue?* he mutters to himself.

As he reflects, the reality of Cynthia's growing control over his life becomes painfully clear. *"Why did I choose her over Chloe in the first place?"* he questions, frustration and regret creeping in. Does Chloe still care about me? And what about Britney? The image of a beautiful girl in a Princeton T-shirt, smiling at him, suddenly flashes in his mind.

His mind spins, the questions and doubts blurring together. Unable to think clearly, Dillon decides he needs a drink to clear his head.

He steps into a nearby bar. It is late afternoon, and the place is nearly empty. As he scans the room, he spots two young women at a bar table, their backs turned to him. It takes only a moment for him to recognize them—Chloe and Britney.

"What are they doing here?" he mutters under his breath.

Hesitant by nature, Dillon considers turning around and leaving. But before he can make his exit, the bartender spots him.

"Dillon! Pre-trial nerves?" the bartender calls out.

He has no idea his shout is about to change everything.

Chloe and Britney quickly turn around, their eyes locking onto Dillon. With no escape, Dillon walks over and says, "Hi, Chloe. Hi, Britney."

He knows he doesn't have much of a choice now.

— ✦ —

Cynthia is sitting across from Kyle in his office, her voice tinged with concern. "Kyle, it seems Dillon is serious about pursuing the compensation. If he takes this to court, what are the chances he'll win?"

Kyle leans back in his chair, a confident smirk on his face. "He won't," he says firmly. "You're his girlfriend — you know him better than anyone. Dillon's not the confrontational type, and he always defers to you. He's not going to cross us." Kyle chuckles darkly. "And if he tries, I'll make sure he regrets it."

Cynthia, still uneasy, presses on. "But if he really does file a lawsuit, what are our chances?"

Kyle's expression hardens as he pounds his fist on the desk. "If it comes to that, our chances aren't great. But we'll make sure it never gets that far."

Dillon slides into the seat next to Chloe and nods at the bartender.
"Put their drinks on my tab," he says casually.

Chloe raises an eyebrow. "No Cynthia today? You two are usually inseparable."

Dillon shakes his head. "Not today. I've been working on a compensation case for Mr. Gonzalez. Just needed a break."

Chloe's expression softens with concern. "Are you sure about this, Dillon? I know Kyle. He's not someone you want to cross lightly. You need to be careful." Her voice carries a note of genuine worry.

Dillon nods. "I will."

He glances toward Britney, noticing she's been unusually quiet—stealing quick looks at him but saying nothing.

He opens his mouth to start a conversation, but Chloe jumps in first.

"It's good to see you here, Dillon," she says with a warm smile. "I just remembered I have an appointment in an hour and need to leave now. Could you give Britney a ride home for me?"

It's clear she's giving them space.

Dillon answers immediately, "Of course. I'd be happy to. See you around, Chloe."

As Dillon drives, he glances at Britney with a mischievous smile and asks, "Is today Daniel's birthday? Why are you out with Chloe at this time of day? Is your family celebrating his birthday?"

Britney responds quickly, "The celebration is this evening. Chloe and I were just out this afternoon picking up a gift for him."

"Really?" Dillon says, and they both laugh.

Suddenly, Britney feels a surge of confidence and decides to seize the moment. "I'm just teasing, Dillon. Is your offer to see *Frozen* still on?" she asks with a daring and hopeful tone. She lets the words fly, unsure if they'll hold.

Dillon blinks in surprise, then a slow smile spreads across his face. "It is if you still want it to be. Let's have an early dinner and see the show."

—✦—

Back in Philadelphia, Fraser sits by Lucia's bedside, furiously typing notes into his laptop.

"Her muscle reactions indicated she could sense the tears of those she loved. Her brainwaves are still very flat, though there are some signs of improvement, albeit faint. The response is far from strong enough to suggest she might awaken soon," he reflects. "If only I could find more people who are emotionally connected to her. Their presence might improve her chances of recovery. But given her tumultuous life, do such people even exist?"

When Fraser returns to his hotel, he calls Kelsi.

"I'm not able to help Lucia regain consciousness," he admits, his voice heavy with disappointment. "I don't know enough about her background to gather the concerned friends and relatives needed."

"Oh, Fritz, don't blame yourself," Kelsi says gently, her voice fills with emotion. "You've done more than most to help already. You've given them hope." She pauses before adding, "By the way, have you spoken with Mr. Liu? Their team has tracked down the marketing connection to the counterfeit company and is hiring Dillon as the plaintiff attorney to sue them. I heard the company is run by the brother of Dillon's girlfriend. You might be called to serve as an expert witness in the case."

"That's good news," Fraser responds. "If we succeed, it will at least bring some compensation to Carlos's family. By the way, how is Brit doing?" He expressed concern for his young sister-in-law, knowing she is bright but still grappling with her emotions.

"Don't worry about her. I'll fill you in when you're back home," Kelsi reassures him warmly.

— ✦ —

After the show, Britney and Dillon make their way to the parking lot. Dillon stops dead. A red X slashes across his windshield, and a note flutters under the wiper blade.

Britney gasps, her eyes wide with shock. Dillon immediately pulls her close, wrapping an arm around her protectively. He retrieves the note, unfolding it to reveal the message: "Mind your own business."

Without hesitation, Dillon says calmly, "This is from Kyle. He's warning me to back off the case."

"Should we report this to the police?" Britney suggests, her voice trembling. She has never dealt with anything like this before.

"It won't do much good," Dillon replies, trying to calm her. "There's no solid proof Kyle did this. To the police, it might just look like a prank. I'll be careful. Let me get you home safely first."

171

They get into the car, and Dillon starts the engine. The big red "**X**" on the windshield partially obstructs his view, but the night is clear. He drives slowly and cautiously, ensuring Britney's safety as they head back.

When they arrive at Fraser's house, Dillon parks the car and walks Britney to the door. Just before she punches in the door code, Dillon gently wraps his arms around her.

"I'm sorry for the scare you had tonight," he whispers, his voice tender and close. "I'll be okay. Thank you for a wonderful evening."

He hesitates for a breath, then leans in and brushes his lips against hers — a soft, searching kiss that says everything words can't.

The faint glow of the X-cross reflected on the windshield glimmers between them, a quiet witness to something new being written in both their hearts.

Britney feels warmth rise through her chest, gentle and steady, like faith finding its way home. She returns his embrace, lingering for a heartbeat before stepping back.

"Please be careful. Good night, Dillon. I'll be there with Fraser — to support you in court."

She offers him a smile that trembles between courage and affection before opening the door and slipping inside.

Dillon sits back in his seat, her kiss lingering like a quiet vow. Whatever tomorrow brings, he wants to meet it with the courage she believes he has.

— ✦ —

It is after ten, and the kids are already asleep. As Britney passes the lounge, she hears the soft strains of piano music drifting through the air.

"Hey, Sis. It's late—why are you playing piano now?" Britney asks as she approaches her sister.

"Oh, Brit, I am waiting for you. Did you have a good time with Chloe today?" Kelsi asks, rising from the piano bench and moving to the couch.

Britney sits close to her sister, excitement bubbling up.

"I talked a lot with Chloe about Dillon today," she says, barely able to contain herself. "She opened up about his background and why he is so indecisive. But the best part? She says it's definitely over between them. She's reconnected with another high school sweetheart, who is also heading to UCLA for his PhD in Engineering."

Kelsi grins and teases, "So that's why you've been smiling like you've won the lottery?"

Britney nods shyly and continues, "Chloe could tell how I felt about Dillon. She's my best friend—she knows me too well. She said Dillon's genuinely a kind and caring person and encouraged me to take a chance." She pauses, a smile playing on her lips. "And just then, Dillon walked into the bar. It felt like fate, so Chloe suggested he drive me home."

Kelsi smirks, catching on quickly. "It's after ten now. Dillon must have been driving really, really slowly," she teases. "Or maybe you two have a few extra stops along the way?"

"We had an early dinner and went to see *Frozen*," Britney replies. "He asked me a few days ago, but I wasn't sure about it." She paused before continuing. "But after the show, we found his car vandalized. Someone painted a red mark on the windshield. Dillon thought it must be Kyle's way of warning him to back off the case."

"Seriously?" Kelsi gasps, shocks that someone would threaten an attorney to drop a case. "How did he react? You mentioned he's usually indecisive and struggles with making firm decisions."

"He is determined to see this through," Britney says, her voice tinged with pride. "He told me that Fritz inspired him to do the right thing. And that he won't be indecisive anymore... he says he is doing this for me." Britney looks down, a blush spreading across her face as she whispers the last part.

Kelsi is touched. Before she could say anything, Britney's phone chimes with a text.

"It's from Dillon," Britney tells her sister. "He'll be out of town for a few days and will show up in court that day."

"That's a smart move," Kelsi praises. "Now we will pray for his safety, and for you two." She adds with a smile.

That night, as Britney lies in bed, the frightening memory of seeing Dillon's car vandalized slowly fades, replaced by the sweet times they've shared over dinner and a movie. Then another memory comes — Chloe folding her arms, watching her with a nervous smile. *"Listen,"* Chloe had said firmly, her voice *cutting through the chatter. "If he ever hurts you, even a little, he'll have to answer to me."* She had tried to soften it with a grin, but her eyes stayed sharp with protective fire.

The thought of Chloe's fierce loyalty warms her. With a faint smile, Britney drifts into a sound sleep.

Chapter 16 *Summertime Reflections*

Precursor of the Real Trial

Fraser slumps against the airplane window, exhausted after a grueling week in Philadelphia. Despite working late every night, he has made frustratingly little progress with his comatose patient.

Perhaps this isn't about curing Lucia at all. Maybe God intends this as preparation — lessons for future cases when the time is right.

Needing a rest, he puts on his headphones and listens to some music. He loves oldies, so he tunes into an oldies station.

"Summertime, and the livin' is easy..."

The familiar melody stirs something deep within him, and a fleeting image of a young woman crosses his mind.

It is George Gershwin's "Summertime", a song that holds a special place in his heart. With a sigh, he shakes his head and skips to the next track.

"...And all the things I ever said, I swear they still are true For no one else can have the part of me I gave to you..."

This time it is Mary MacGregor's "Torn Between Two Lovers". He has heard that tune countless times before, but this time the melody strikes a deep chord in his heart. The same woman's image reappears, more persistent this time.

"For no one else can have the part of me I give to you... Is that true?" he wonders, recalling the dark days of depression he had faced after graduation and how he was ultimately saved by the grace of his Lord.

"Why am I thinking about her now? It has been over ten years since we lost touch. The sudden memory makes no sense!" He tries to push the thoughts away, but emotions have a way of creeping back uninvited. Some memories don't fade; they stalk you, no matter where you go.

"Could she be in trouble? Does she need help?" The thought suddenly occurs to him. *"But what can I do? We lost contact years ago. How could I possibly help her now?"*

He sighs, shaking his head in frustration, and switches off the music.

— ✦ —

Kelsi and Britney are waiting at arrivals when Fraser emerges from the gate, leaving Nanny Rose home with the children. Before they even reach home, the sisters fill Fraser in on everything that has happened.

"How are you feeling, Brit? Is your head clearer now?" Fraser's voice is mixed with gentle caring.

"Yes," Britney replies shyly, "but I'm still afraid that Dillon is going up against Cynthia's brother. Chloe mentioned that Kyle can be rough—sometimes even violent. I'm scared he might try to hurt Dillon." Her voice is filled with genuine worry.

Hearing her concern, Kelsi chimes in. "Jiang Industries has a security team. I'll ask Mr. Liu to reach out to them, just in case the police won't take action."

Hearing her sister's suggestion, Britney finally smiles, feeling a bit more reassured.

When they arrive home, Fraser immediately picks up the phone and calls Dr. Stephens.

"Colin? It's Fraser. I just got back from Philadelphia. I'll meet you at your Stanford lab tomorrow at noon. I've got some intriguing observations about a coma patient that I need to share with you." His voice buzzes with excitement. "Oh, and yes, I'll pass the message along," he adds with a smile before hanging up.

"You really should rest before meeting Colin, Fritz," Kelsi suggests, but she knows him all too well: *rest can wait;*

inspiration can't. Once his mind is set, there's no turning him aside.

"What's got you smiling like that?" she asks, curious about the last part of his conversation.

"Oh, by the way, Brit, Colin asked me to thank you for having lunch with him. He really enjoyed it and hopes to see you again sometime," Fraser replies, revealing the message from Colin with a knowing smile.

Britney simply stays silent, a deep smile spreading across her face — a response that isn't typical of her. Kelsi notices and realizes that her sister's thoughts are entirely occupied by Dillon, and nothing else seems to matter.

— ✦ —

Fraser has a long session with Colin, discussing his findings from his in-depth study of Lucia in Philadelphia. Before he leaves, they grab some coffee and chat in the Stanford cafeteria.

"How's Britney?" Colin asks.

"She's fine." Fraser hesitates somewhat. "I see that you really like her, but I have to tell you her heart seems to be with somebody else."

"Is that the attorney she told me about, in the lawsuit over the victim of '*Eyes of an Angel*'?" His gaze fixes on the shadows stretching across the courtyard outside the cafeteria. "I know she'd never really be mine," he says softly, almost to himself. "But knowing doesn't make it hurt any less." He forces a small smile and shakes his head. "Still, she deserves to follow her heart. That's all I ever wanted for her." To him, real love is love choosing dignity instead of possession.

Fraser studies him for a moment, moved by the calm conviction beneath his words. In Colin's composure, he sees not weakness, but the kind of grace that only love can teach.

Two days pass quickly, and it is now the day of the trial. Fraser, Britney, and Mr. Liu's patent team head to the courthouse, while Kelsi stays home with the kids.

As Britney enters the courtroom, she spots Chloe and takes a seat beside her. Moments later, Dillon walks in. It has been a few days since they last saw him, and he looks noticeably pale and thinner.

Across the aisle, Kyle sits with a smirk on his face. Cynthia is seated at the far end among the spectators.

The trial proceeds fairly quickly. After both the plaintiff and defendant attorneys had presented their cases, Fraser is called to the stand. He provides evidence that the "*Eyes of an Angel*" product used by Mr. Gonzalez is a knockoff, not the patented version from Jiang Industries.

It doesn't take long for the jury to reach a verdict.

"We, the jury, find the defendant guilty."

"The court finds in favor of the plaintiff. The defendant is ordered to pay one hundred thousand dollars in damages," the judge declares, striking the gavel on the sound block. "Case dismissed."

As everyone begins to leave the courtroom, Britney can't contain herself. She rushes toward Dillon and wraps him in a big hug. Fraser and Chloe follow close behind, extending their hands to Dillon. "Congratulations!" "Well done!" they say, smiling.

Still embracing Britney, Dillon catches sight of Kyle and Cynthia leaving the courtroom, their faces twisted with disgust. A sense of unease washes over him. Even in the noise of victory, something about their silence unnerves him.

Even though Britney clearly wants to stay with him, Dillon gently pulls back and says, "Britney, I need to follow up with Fraser on something related to the case. Chloe, could you please take Britney home first?" He turns to Chloe with a request.

"Of course. We'll catch up with you later," Chloe replies, guiding Britney toward her car as they walk away.

Fraser turns to Mr. Liu. "Many thanks to your team for helping us win this case. I believe we're in the clear now. "He nods at the two men standing behind Mr. Liu, who are clearly members of Jiang Industries' security team.

As they step outside, Fraser says to Dillon, "A hundred thousand dollars isn't much when it comes to covering medical bills for a coma patient. I'd like to double that amount from our foundation's funds."

"That's incredibly generous of you, Fraser," Dillon replies, starting to address Fraser by his first name. He nods to him with respect as they reach Dillon's car.

— ✦ —

"The court case should be over by now. Have we won the case?" Kelsi mumbles to herself as she finishes changing the kids. She picks up her phone and calls Fraser, but he isn't answering.

"Oh, they all must have gone for a drink to celebrate. But Fritz always returns my calls." She starts to worry as she thinks of Fraser being stabbed and saved by Jordan five years ago. She turns on the television.

"Breaking news from Channel 5. A drive-by shooting on Highway 880 has left two men in critical condition after their car plunged into a canyon. The vehicle has been identified as a 2020 white Nissan Altima sedan. The driver has been identified as Mr. Dillon Jung, an attorney who had just completed a court case in Oakland earlier this afternoon," the anchorwoman reports.

Kelsi is in shock. *"Dillon is shot? Is Britney in the car with him? Is she okay?"* She knows all too well how deeply her sister cares for Dillon and is certain they are together.

The news continues, "One passenger was in the vehicle with Mr. Jung. He has been identified as Mr. Fraser Lin, the son-in-law of Mr. Jiang from Jiang Industries. Both were transported to U.C. Medical Center and are in critical condition."

Kelsi freezes.

She remembers another night like this—the call about Patrick, the stillness that followed, the ache of not knowing what tomorrow would hold. She had Fraser then to hold her through the fear. But now the fear cuts deeper, sharper, because it carries Fraser's name.

She collapses onto the couch, breathless, as if the news itself has stolen the air from her lungs.

Grief doesn't knock—it barges in.

And this time, it arrives with Britney and Chloe.

"We just heard—Dillon was shot and his car went off the canyon! And Fritz is with him! What happened? How could they end up in a canyon? Why is Fritz with him?" Britney cries, her voice rising to a hysterical pitch.

Chloe pulls Britney into a calming embrace, guiding her down to sit, and keeps her own fear quiet.

Seeing Britney unravel and Kelsi barely holding herself upright, Chloe finally steps in.

"Let's go to U.C. Medical Center and find out exactly what's happening. I'll drive."

Calm and collected as always, Chloe becomes the anchor Kelsi and Britney desperately need.

When they arrive at the hospital, they are surprised to see Colin already there, speaking with a doctor.

Seeing Colin, Britney and Kelsi feel an unexpected sense of calm. Perhaps they hope he can work miracles, just as Fraser often does.

After the doctor steps away, Colin turns to the Jiang sisters, nodding solemnly. "Both Fraser and Dillon are still in critical condition," he begins. "There were three shots fired, and Dillon was hit twice—once in the left shoulder and once in the right chest, narrowly missing vital organs."

He looks at Britney gently before continuing. "The gunshots weren't fatal, but when the car plummeted, the sunroof was fully open. A thick branch struck the car." Colin sighs heavily. "Although they were both wearing seatbelts, the branch hit them both on the head."

As Colin speaks, a doctor approaches the group.

"Is one of you Mrs. Lin? I'm Dr. Jennings, overseeing the cases of Mr. Jung and Mr. Lin," he introduces himself, his gaze shifting between the three women.

"I'm Kelsi Lin, Fraser's wife. How are Fraser and Dillon? Can we see them?" Kelsi quickly steps forward. She has regained her composure now that they are inside the hospital.

"Not yet. We've removed the bullets from Mr. Jung's body, and he's currently receiving a blood transfusion. Is either of you related to Mr. Jung?" Dr. Jennings turns to Chloe and Britney.

Before Britney can respond, Chloe speaks up, "No, we're just friends. Have his family been notified?"

"Not yet. We've had difficulty locating his relatives," Dr. Jennings replies, a note of frustration in his voice.

Chloe nods thoughtfully. "I know his parents moved back to Korea two years ago. He has an older sister, but she's out of state. I've never met her," she adds, drawing on what she knows as Dillon 's ex-girlfriend.

"What's their condition now?" Britney asks, her voice trembling, tears welling up in her eyes. "When can we see them?"

"The branch that came through the sunroof caused severe head trauma to both men," Dr. Jennings explains. "Mr. Jung is experiencing shock that has temporarily affected his vision. He may have lost his sight for now, but we expect it to return within three to four days." He then turns to Kelsi with a more somber expression. "As for Mr. Lin, his situation is a bit more complicated."

Dr. Jennings takes a breath before continuing. "It appears Mr. Lin wasn't as well restrained as Dillon — his seatbelt may not have been positioned properly during the crash. That could explain why he seems to have taken the harder hit. We don't see any serious external injuries, but he's still unconscious. We'll do a full scan tonight to better understand why."

"You may see them in an hour, but your visit should be short." Having said these words, Dr. Jennings leaves.

They gather in the hospital lounge, trying to relax a bit before seeing the two patients.

185

"This must be Kyle's doing," Chloe says, losing her calm. "I knew he might seek revenge, but I never imagined he'd go so far as to shoot."

"Let's not worry about Kyle right now. The authorities will handle that," Kelsi says, trying to keep her voice steady. "Our focus should be on Fritz. Colin, why would someone remain unconscious if there were no visible injuries?" She turns to Dr. Stephens for answers.

"Brain trauma can be difficult to detect," Colin explains." It's only been a few hours, and trauma like this takes time to heal. We just have to hope for improvement in the coming days."

They head to Fraser's room. But on the way, Britney insists on stopping by Dillon's room first.

When they reach Dillon's door, they find him lying in bed, a bandage covering his eyes and an IV line attached to his arm. Britney moves to rush in, but Kelsi gently holds her back and signals for Chloe to go in first.

As Chloe quietly approaches Dillon's bedside, the faint rhythm of the heart monitor fills the room. Dillon stirs, his voice barely above a whisper. "Britney, I'll be fine. Don't worry." Though he can't see who is coming, he instinctively calls out Britney's name—some recognitions don't need sight.

Chloe stops a few steps away, the sound of his words catching her breath. For a moment, she just stands there, torn between sorrow and understanding, realizing that even in his pain, his heart still knows where it belongs.

186

In that moment, they all realize that the place Chloe once held in Dillon's heart now belongs entirely to Britney. Britney rushes to his bedside and takes his hands in hers.

Chloe, Kelsi, and Colin quietly step back outside the patient room.

Kelsi glances at Colin to see his reaction.

"Oh, I love that girl," Colin says with a smile. "She's so direct and unafraid to show how she feels. She likes Dillon, and she's not shy about expressing it." His words are warm and sincere, without a trace of jealousy.

Chloe realizes there's no reason to stay—this moment clearly isn't hers anymore. She glances at her watch. "I have to go now—I have an early appointment tomorrow. Dr. Stephens, could you take them home later?" she asks Colin.

"No problem. We'll stay a little longer. I need to learn more about Fraser's condition," Colin responds promptly.

As they walk toward Fraser's room, Kelsi muses aloud, "Why was Fraser in Dillon's car? If they were celebrating, they didn't need to go that far."

"Knowing Fraser, he probably needed something important from Dillon, but Dillon didn't have it with him, so they went back to get it," Colin speculates. As Fraser's partner and close friend, Colin is well acquainted with how Fraser thinks.

They enter Fraser's room and find him lying motionless in bed, electrodes connecting his body to a CRT monitor.

187

Colin glances at the screen, noting the steady but weak heartbeat.

Kelsi hurries to Fraser's bedside, taking in the slight furrow between his brows and the soft smile that somehow remains on his lips. She wraps her arms around his neck, her silent tears falling onto his still face.

She keeps vigil with the patience of prayer, clinging to hope the way a soul clings to faith — quietly, fiercely, as though her belief alone might call him back to life. The faint rhythm of his breathing and heartbeat feel like prayer waiting to be answered.

Chapter 17 *Unfinished Clues*

The Keys to Heal

჻ ჻ ჻

The next morning, Kelsi and Britney make their way to the courthouse parking lot to collect Fraser's abandoned SUV.

As Britney opens the car door, she spots a sticky note on the driver's seat: *"Ask Dillon about Gonzalez — what happens in their family before the accident"*

"This must be why Fritz was in Dillon's car yesterday," Britney says, showing the note to her sister.

"What could be so important?"

Kelsi glances at the note. "Fritz mentioned he couldn't help Mrs. Gonzalez to regain consciousness, right before he left Philadelphia. It seems like he uncovered something new yesterday — something crucial for him to continue pursuing to help her out of the coma." She completely understands Fraser's determination.

When they return home, Kelsi invites Colin over and shows him Fraser's note.

"What could have happened in Gonzalez's family before the accident?" Colin asks as they discuss the situation together. "Fraser is researching coma patients' brainwaves. I'll review his notes for clues." He pauses, thoughtful. "Sometimes the data can't tell us everything. But maybe Fraser saw something we haven't yet."

In the afternoon, Kelsi and Britney visit the U. C. Medical Center again. With Dillon slowly regaining his strength but still unable to see, Britney spends most of her time by his side, feeding him and reading him whatever he likes to hear.

Meanwhile, Kelsi remains in Fraser's room. After years of witnessing his unwavering faith, she kneels beside his bed, holding his hands as she prays. She knows God wouldn't take someone the world still needs. In the silence, she clings to faith's hand when no one else can answer.

— ✦ —

At Stanford Hospital, Colin sits beside a comatose patient, absorbed in his work. His eyes move between his monitor and Fraser's laptop while he occasionally checks the patient's vitals and facial movements.

Finally, Colin pauses, nodding to himself as he closes Fraser's laptop. A slight smile appears on his face.

He drives to U. C. Medical Center and meets with Dr. Jennings, an old colleague he has known for years. Both are leaders in their fields and hold each other in high regard.

"What exactly happened to Fraser?" he asks. "Have you found any clues as to why he's comatose when Dillon, who sustained even more injuries, is likely to fully recover?"

Dr. Jennings frowns. "The car rolled several times—the impact centered on the driver's side, so Fraser took the worst of it. But there's more."

He pulls out a report and hands it to Colin. "The brain scan revealed an old head injury and signs of past severe depression—both affect consciousness. And Fraser's brain... it's not typical." Dr. Jennings sighs heavily. "At this stage, all we can do is wait."

"May I spend a few hours with him in his room?" Colin asks sadly. "It's ironic—recently our work has been focused on helping comatose patients, and now he's become one. I'll let you know if I discover anything."

When Colin enters Fraser's room, he finds Kelsi and Britney standing by the bedside, their eyes brimming with tears. He notices the exhaustion and worry etched on their faces, so he approaches them gently.

"Let's take a break and sit down in the cafeteria. There's something important I need to discuss with you," he suggests earnestly.

They find a quiet table in the cafeteria and sit down. Colin places his laptop on the table between them.

"I had a long talk with Fraser after he returned," Colin begins, his tone serious. "He told me that when Lucia's face — that is,

Mrs. Gonzalez's — was touched by her family's tears, he found a slight reaction. Even more interesting, when he synchronized her heartbeat with her children's, there was a positive response. However, there was no such response when he tried the same with her husband."

Kelsi looks puzzled, while Britney quickly jumps in, "Wait, he discovered that a comatose patient can actually respond to their loved ones? That's amazing!" She turns to her sister, her excitement growing. "This could be the key to helping him!"

"Hold on, Britney," Colin says cautiously. "Fraser mentioned that the responses were so subtle, he wasn't sure if this 'emotional energy' would be strong enough to bring a patient out of a coma. But it's definitely worth a shot. I'll develop a procedure and see where it leads us."

Kelsi's eyes light up upon hearing this. "Thank you so much, Colin. I'll bring Tiffany and Daniel tomorrow. They both mean so much to Fraser."

The next morning, Kelsi asks Nanny Rose to bring Tiffany and Daniel along with her and Britney to the hospital. When they arrive, they find Colin setting up a table and computers, preparing for the experiment.

"The key parameter we're looking for is a strong, consistent heartbeat from Fraser. His brain needs sufficient oxygen to start directing his body to respond. Right now, his heartbeat is just too weak." Colin explains his procedure in simple terms.

"Britney, I need you to help me synchronize the heartbeats of Tiffany, Daniel, and Kelsi with Fraser's, one at a time. I'll use the smart wedding rings to tap into his inner thoughts and see if we can trigger a reaction."

Colin demonstrates the process to Britney, and the Princeton graduate quickly grasps the instructions.

An hour has passed, and Colin shakes his head in frustration.

"I can sense the emotional energy increase every time one of you touches him," he says, "but the difference isn't strong enough to make a significant impact. When all three of you touch him together, it's getting closer, but still not enough." Colin sighs, wondering what *enough* even means.

Kelsi, holding Daniel in her arms, is at a loss for words. As Colin's words sink in, tears stream down her face, falling onto Daniel's cheeks. Feeling his mother's tears, Daniel begins to cry. Tiffany, sensing the sadness, wraps her little arms around Kelsi's leg and starts crying too.

The tears fall onto Fraser's face, some landing on his lips.

Colin's eyes widen as he feels the energy shift—growing, intensifying—only to stop short. It's stronger than before, but still cannot cross the threshold.

He turns to Kelsi and says, "Let's take a break. Maybe Rose can take the kids home to rest; this has been really hard on them. And I need to discuss something with you."

The three of them sit at a table in the cafeteria.

"I believe Fraser's theory is on the right track," Colin begins. "The emotional energy is real, but it has to be strong enough to reach his brain." He sighs. "You three are the most important people in his life, and yet the transmitted energy still falls short. What else can we try? Is there anyone else who means as much to him as you three?"

"Sarah!" Kelsi and Britney exclaim in unison.

"Who's Sarah? Is she Fraser's girlfriend?" Colin asks, puzzled. Kelsi then starts telling him the story of Sarah, from before she and Fraser are married.

Colin nods and asks, "Are you still in touch with Sarah? Do you think you can explain the situation to her and ask her to come?"

Kelsi replies, "She married Jordan four years ago, and I heard they had a two-year-old daughter now. She's been busy with her family, so we haven't spoken in two years. But I'll call her. I'm sure if she hears about Fraser's accident, she'll come."

Britney recalls what Fraser has told her about Sarah. "If Sarah can come and help, I'm certain it'll make a difference," she says with a hopeful smile.

— ✦ —

Sarah is playing with her daughter when Kelsi calls.

"Oh, Kelsi! How have you been? Keeping busy with the kids? How's Fraser?" she greets Kelsi warmly.

"We're doing okay, Sarah, but Fraser isn't," Kelsi replies in a somber tone. She then briefly explains what has happened. "Can you come see him? It's really important." She decides to save Colin's suggestion for when they meet in person.

Hearing that Fraser is in a coma, Sarah is stunned. "How could something like this happen to such a kind person? Of course, I'll come. I'll be there tomorrow morning." Her connection with Fraser is like old threads: they don't break — they braid together.

After hanging up, she kneels in front of the cross on her kitchen wall and prays.

"Our Lord, You allow everything to happen for a reason. We may not understand why You've let Fraser go through this, but please grant us the faith to guide us through and to learn Your will. Amen."

The next morning, Sarah arrives at the hospital. As soon as Kelsi sees her, she steps forward and gives her a warm embrace.

"Sarah, it's been years! You look as beautiful as ever. How are Jordan and the little one?" Kelsi asks warmly.

195

"Jordan's on assignment in China for a month, and my parents are watching Audrey at home," Sarah replies. Then she turns to Britney with a smile. "You must be Britney! I haven't seen you in five years, and now you're as beautiful—even taller than your sister!" She gently pats Britney on the shoulder.

Britney glances at her, wanting to say something but holding back.

As they make their way to the patient's room, Kelsi leans a little closer to Sarah.

"How are Katie and Charlie doing? Are they adjusting to school? Any challenges?" She lowers her voice. "They're so different from the other kids… I just want to make sure they're okay."

Sarah smiles softly. "They're doing better than you think. Katie's getting really good at speeches and still helps Charlie with his reading. And Charlie's phys-ed teacher says he's showing real confidence — he's even learning to shoot baskets, can you believe it? They still have rough days, but they're finding their rhythm."

Kelsi exhales, relieved. "Good. Fraser always worries about them."

Sarah nods. "I know. They're part of his heart."

When they enter Fraser's room, they find Colin inside, preparing and getting things ready.

"Good morning, Colin. This is our good friend, Sarah Tran," Kelsi begins the introductions, "and this is Dr. Stephens. Dr. Stephens is a close friend and colleague of Fritz's, and he's also familiar with his research."

"Nice to meet you, Dr. Stephens." After shaking Colin's hand, Sarah approaches Fraser's bed. She sees him lying there, motionless, but with a gentle smile on his face — the same smile she remembers when he first sees his '*Eyes of an Angel*' successfully helping Charlie, just as he has envisioned.

She steps closer, reaching out to grasp Fraser's hands. Colin notices her eyes gradually welling up with tears. She remains silent, but the emotion in her eyes speaks volumes.

"This might be the right person," Colin thinks to himself. Knowing that Kelsi must have already explained the situation to her, he decides not to waste time repeating the details. Instead, he gets straight to the point.

"Miss Sarah, before Fraser fell into a coma, he was researching ways to help coma patients regain consciousness. Isn't that ironic?" Colin begins. "His notes suggest that a coma patient might subconsciously tap into some sort of inexplicable energy—I call it emotional energy—from someone they share a strong emotional bond with. If that energy is powerful enough, it could potentially wake up the brain." He simplifies the explanation, making it easy to understand even for a layperson.

"Oh, he was working on helping coma patients when this happened? He's always been focusing on using his God-given

197

talents to help others. But why would God let this happen to him?" Sarah leans over Fraser, her fingers gently closing around his.

Her tears—quiet, unwilling, full of years she never said aloud—slip down and fall onto his lips.

A tremor flickers across Fraser's eyelids.

Kelsi stiffens.

Britney inhales sharply.

Even Sarah draws in a breath she doesn't mean to make.

On the monitor, a faint lift appears—small but unmistakable.

Colin immediately swivels toward the screen. "Britney—come here." His voice is urgent, low, focused.

Britney moves to Fraser's other side and follows his direction. Colin adjusts readings, compares baselines, watches the pattern rise—build—almost crest—then settle just short of where it needs to go.

He exhales slowly and closes the laptop.

"Sarah's presence definitely amplifies the emotional energy. What we just saw—that spike—that's the strongest response so far."

He turns to the three women with a mixture of relief and frustration. "But even then, it still isn't enough to push his brain into consciousness."

Kelsi wipes her eyes. "So... what else can we do?"

Colin hesitates before answering. "There's a limit to how far emotional resonance can travel. When someone's this deep in a coma, the bond has to be very powerful—*family-level* powerful." He gives a helpless shrug. "We may need someone else from his family."

"I know his father passed away when he was young. His mother is eighty now and has Alzheimer's; she's in a long-term care facility," Kelsi shares what she knows. "His oldest brother died from a stroke and heart attack a few years ago. He has two sisters—one is battling stage three colon cancer, and the other is working in Taiwan. It's unlikely any of them could come."

"Then let's take a break and figure out our next steps," Colin tells everyone.

Britney feels helpless seeing Fraser still motionless. She needs air—needs hope—so she slips quietly toward Dillon's room.

Inside, she finds him sitting on his bed, listening to a news broadcast.

"Is that you, Brit?" he calls out, using the affectionate nickname her family uses.

Britney quickly steps forward and embraces him. "How are you feeling, Dillon? What would you like to do now?"

With a swift motion, Dillon raises his left hand and pulls off the bandage over his eyes. "I want to see your beautiful face right now!" he says as he presses his lips against hers. For him, sight returns first through the heart.

"You can see?" Britney exclaims, wrapping her arms around his neck in joy.

As they savor the moment, a young woman doctor enters the room. Noticing Dillon has a visitor, she introduces herself politely. "I'm Dr. Summer Tang, Dillon's ophthalmologist for this case. Sorry to interrupt, but I need to check his eyes one more time to ensure everything's fine before he's cleared."

Britney sits quietly in a corner of the room as Dr. Tang uses an ophthalmoscope to examine Dillon's eyes. After finishing the exam, she moves to the computer and begins typing her notes.

"Over the past few days, Colin has tried to involve everyone Fritz knows to help him regain consciousness, but it hasn't worked," Britney summarizes Fraser's situation for Dillon.

"It's really unfortunate how things have turned out. Fraser Lin is the kindest person I've ever met. He even offered to double the compensation for the Gonzalez family," Dillon responds with a heavy heart.

"Fraser Lin? Is that him?" Dr. Tang murmurs to herself when she overhears the name as she types. Her hand pauses above the keyboard, though she isn't sure why. The mention of Fraser's name stirs something deep within her—like a pebble dropped into still water, sending quiet ripples across her heart.

Chapter 18 *Love and Miracles*

The Angels Among Us

৶ ৶ ৶

In the cafeteria, Colin explains his recent attempts to Kelsi and Sarah.

"I can definitely feel Miss Sarah's presence making a difference," Colin says, reflecting on his recent efforts. "I tried so hard to channel that surge of energy toward Fraser's eyes and lips, but I came up just a bit short. No matter how much I pushed, I couldn't quite get it over the hump," he explains, referring to his experience while wearing the smart wedding ring.

"If it's God's will for us to wait, then we must be patient and trust in His guidance," Sarah says softly, clasping her hands together." He always has a plan."

"Yes, that's all we can do," Colin agrees. "By the way, I've noticed something interesting—this emotional energy seems strongest when the connection between the patient and the other person is very recent. If there hasn't been any emotional connection for, say, more than six months, the energy becomes barely detectable and isn't effective anymore," he explains as Britney enters the cafeteria. They wave her over to join them.

"Dillon's vision is back!" Britney eagerly announces." He's resting now and will be discharged tomorrow morning."

"That's great news! But what about Kyle? He is still after him," Kelsi asks with concern.

"Not anymore!" Britney responds cheerfully. "Dillon kept hearing updates, and he told me the police had apprehended Kyle and his gang. They're in custody now."

Sarah, still reflecting on Colin's earlier words, suddenly speaks up. "I haven't been in contact with Fraser for a couple of years." She turns to Colin and says thoughtfully, "If that's true, you shouldn't have sensed anything between us at all."

Before Colin could respond, Britney jumps in. "I think what Colin says is true. Sis Sarah, I had a chat with Fritz a couple of weeks ago about his past, before he married my sister." She looks at Sarah with a warm smile. "He mentioned you, and I could feel the deep affection he still had for you. Our conversation might have stirred some of those strong emotional feelings within him."

Sarah blushes slightly, unsure of how to respond. Kelsi gently takes her hand and adds, "We all know Fritz. He's a man driven by his emotions—emotions that inspire him to do great things. And we're proud we all are a part of that."

— ✦ —

After Dr. Tang goes back to her office, she looks up Fraser Lin's patient information.

"That's him," she sighs, her thoughts drifting back to that day ten years ago. She remembers flunking her midterm and sobbing in his arms, how he gently ran his hand through her hair, murmuring in his off-key voice.

"Summer Tang, and the livin' is easy..."

The tune was so tenderly out of tune that her tears turned into laughter. Then he handed her a cup of hot water—he knew she always preferred it to cold—to calm her down, dabbing a tissue against her cheeks so tenderly that the memory of her Fraser softens, but never fades.

"Now he's married with two children. So, the pretty girl in Dillon's room is his sister-in-law," she murmurs to herself. *"He's living a happily married life. Should I even think about resurfacing in his world?"*

She pauses, her emotions swirling. *"But he's in a coma now... does any of this even matter anymore?"* Her eyes begin to well up with tears. She takes a sip of hot water from the cup on her desk.

That night, after visiting hours, she quietly steps into Fraser's room. Approaching his bed, she gazes at his motionless form, noting the faint, familiar smile still lingering on his lips.

It has been over ten years since she last saw him, and now she studies every feature of his face, as if trying to recapture the time they have lost.

"Do you know I was bluffing back then?" she whispers to the unconscious Fraser, voice barely audible even to herself. "I was lying about Parker. I wanted you to fight for me, to tell me not to go. But you never understood what I needed... I hated you for that."

Her mind drifts back to that day on the beach, sitting together on a rock. She had told him she was going to get engaged to Parker, maybe even get married after graduation. He held her hand, staring into her eyes for what felt like an eternity. Then, after a long, silent pause, he let go, nodded, and simply said, "Good luck."

Tears well up in her eyes. "If only you had hugged me, kissed me then... everything could've been different," she whispers, her voice trembling. Unable to hold back any longer, she leans down and presses her lips against his, her tears falling onto his cheeks.

In that moment, she forgets that everything is being captured on the surveillance camera.

The next morning, while Kelsi and Britney arrive to help Dillon with his discharge, Colin heads to Fraser's room to check on him.

As soon as he puts on the smart wedding ring, he feels the emotional energy surge once more. Alarmed and hopeful, he quickly calls Kelsi to come over.

Taking a closer look at Fraser, he notices faint traces of tears on his face and a subtle lipstick imprint on his lips. Much to his surprise, he also sees tears gathered at the corners of Fraser's closed eyes.

He draws a quiet breath. Something—or someone—reached him... something deeper than any of their earlier attempts.

When Kelsi steps into the room, Colin turns toward her, excitement rising in his voice.

"Please call Sarah immediately! I'm not sure what happened, but Fraser's emotional energy spiked last night. I think we might finally be able to push it over the edge and revive him!"

Moments later, Kelsi, Sarah, and Britney gather in Fraser's room. Dillon is instructed to synchronize the heartbeats of the three women with Fraser's, while Colin closes his eyes, focusing intently on channeling the emotional energy toward Fraser's eyes and lips—his two facial features most likely to show the earliest signs of consciousness.

Suddenly, Fraser's lips move.

"Thirsty," he whispers, the word barely audible.

In that moment, the smallest word carries the heaviest news.

Upon hearing his voice, Kelsi rushes to him and wraps her arms around his neck. "Oh—you're awake now? Brit, give him some water."

Britney hurries in with a cup and straw, while Kelsi gently sits him up and holds the cup so he can sip.

"Hot water," Fraser murmurs, slowly opening his eyes.

"Oh—Brit, warm up the cup." Kelsi remembers how he sometimes sips hot water instead of coffee when he's deep in thought, though she's never asked why.

Fraser looks at Kelsi, then at Britney and Dillon, quiet recognition lighting his tired eyes. When his gaze reaches Sarah, something flickers—memory, relief, or maybe both.

He tries to speak, but the words falter before they can leave his lips.

Sarah steps closer, her breath catching as she kneels beside the bed.

She reaches out, hesitates for a heartbeat, then takes his hand in both of hers. "Don't talk," she whispers. "You're safe now." Her voice trembles with a grace that only love and prayer can shape.

Kelsi watches from the other side, her hand still resting lightly on Fraser's shoulder, steadying him as though holding him between two worlds—the one he's fought to return to and the one that nearly took him away.

And to Fraser, through the haze of weakness, it feels as if both women reached into the dark and pulled him back into the light... with the help of an unspoken angel pushing from behind.

From where he stands, Colin observes in silence, the moment unfolding like a prayer answered. He exchanges a glance with Dillon—both men sensing that something beyond medicine has stirred in this room.

The monitors show only slight improvement, yet what they witness feels far greater: life choosing to return, drawn by the voices and the faith of those who love him.

Fraser exhales softly, his eyelids fluttering closed once more. Kelsi smooths a strand of hair from his forehead as Sarah bows her head in quiet prayer.

Beside them, Britney presses a hand to her chest, her breath trembling. She's not a woman of strong faith—not yet—but seeing Fraser awaken, even for a moment, gives her a kind of strength she's never felt before.

For the first time, she feels faith not as an idea, but as a presence.

Around them, the room settles into a reverent stillness—the kind that follows when a miracle doesn't announce itself, but simply happens.

After a brief pause, Colin steps aside and calls Dr. Jennings to share the unexpected news.

Moments later, Dr. Jennings comes in with a nurse. When he sees Fraser resting in a different posture and Kelsi holding a cup of water beside him, a look of heartfelt astonishment crosses his face.

"Mr. Lin can drink now? What have you done, Colin?" he says with a laugh, both teasing and admiring. "You're welcome to work in our hospital anytime!" Then, more gently, he adds, "But for now, he needs rest. We'll keep him under observation for a few days. Mrs. Lin—congratulations. You can finally sleep well tonight." He nods warmly to Kelsi and to the others before stepping aside to check Fraser's chart.

The five of them sit in the cafeteria again, delighted that Fraser finally regains consciousness. Colin starts sharing his thoughts.

"What really happened last night?" Colin muses aloud. "I think we're at a dead end, with no one else to call for help. Yet this morning I noticed traces of tears on his face, a faint lipstick imprint on his lips, and his eyes were still a bit wet. It looks like someone visited him, shed tears, and kissed him."

"Tears of an angel!" Britney exclaims with a playful grin. "Looks like there's another angel in Fraser's life besides you, Sis Sarah!"

Colin nods thoughtfully. "That's exactly what we needed. But who could that person be? Fraser must have responded to someone with a deep emotional bond."

"The only person I can think of is his ex-girlfriend from college, but that was over ten years ago," Kelsi says, recalling what Fraser had shared with her. "After she left him, he was deeply depressed for a year and only found solace through his faith when he joined the church."

"But it's been ten years; the emotional connection would have faded by now. How would she even know he is here and in this condition?" Colin wonders aloud.

Sarah gently replies, "Our Lord has a way of making things happen in unexpected ways. It seems she was here last night, even if we don't understand how. The Lord often sends help through unexpected means." She reflects on how Kelsi has come through when she needs support to save Charlie.

Knowing that Fraser is now awake and under medical care, Kelsi and Britney take Dillon home while Sarah leaves to share the good news with Jordan. Colin remains at the hospital, intrigued by the mystery of the woman who has visited Fraser.

He heads to the nurse's station, where all patient rooms are monitored 24/7, and requests to view the video footage from Fraser's room the previous night. Given that Colin is a colleague of Dr. Jennings and has been involved in Fraser's case for several days, the nurse agrees to show him the footage.

Colin watches as a doctor enters Fraser's room around ten o'clock. "Who is that doctor?" he inquires.

"She's Dr. Summer Tang, a neuro-ophthalmologist from the Ophthalmology Department," the nurse replies.

The video shows Dr. Tang approaching Fraser's bed, staying for a few minutes, leaning down to kiss him, and then stepping out. Noticing the nurse's giggling reaction, Colin turns to her and says politely, "Please keep this private. It's a matter of confidentiality."

— ✦ —

It has been a long day for Colin, but he is thrilled that his close friend has come out of a coma. All he wants now is a quick dinner before heading home to rest.

The cafeteria is nearly empty, and Colin notices a woman doctor sitting alone, her name tag reading "Dr. Summer Tang". Not wanting to miss this opportunity, he grabs his dinner tray and approaches her. "May I sit here? I hope you're not waiting for anyone," he says politely.

Dr. Tang, surprised that someone would ask to join her when there are so many empty tables around, nods and replies, "Sure, be my guest."

She recalls how, in her younger days, many men were drawn to her, and she's quietly pleased to realize that some things haven't changed.

What she doesn't realize is that the table they share is an altar in disguise.

"Hi, I'm Dr. Stephens. I'm here to help a patient—and a close friend—recover from a coma." Rather than offer a formal introduction, he leads with purpose, hoping to capture her attention.

"Comatose patients?" Dr. Tang looks up sharply. "Wait… are you the Dr. Stephens who published that recent report on brainwave connections with coma patients?" Her tone reveals a woman who keeps up with research far beyond her specialty.

"Yes, that's me," Colin replies. "Fraser Lin is my friend, and this morning I noticed he's becoming responsive—slowly, but clearly recovering."

He watches Dr. Tang's expression shift.

"Oh, he is? How wonderful!" she exclaims—too quickly, too brightly. "But yesterday he seemed motionless…" The words slip out before she can stop them. Her lips press together as she realizes her mistake.

"Dr. Tang," Colin says gently, "you must be a close friend of his."

A faint, embarrassed nod confirms it.

He continues, "Let me tell you what we've been trying. Honestly, nothing was working… until this morning. After your visit last night." He summarizes the events of the past few days.

When he finishes, Dr. Tang draws a breath. "Thank you for sharing this, Dr. Stephens. Yes… Fraser and I were college sweethearts. I even hoped we'd get married."

She sighs, the past rising in her eyes like a tide she hadn't expected to face today.

"Please, call me Colin," he replies. "What happened between you two, Dr. Tang? Did you drift apart, or was it a decision on your end?"

"Call me Summer, please," she says with a faint smile. "We misunderstood each other back then. I didn't grasp his passive nature and pushed him to make a decision. He didn't realize I was bluffing, and he let me go. My pride kept me from going back to him."

For reasons she can't explain, Summer finds herself trusting Colin with feelings she hasn't voiced in years. "I moved to Canada to pursue my M.D., and during that time, I lost touch with him."

"It's quite a coincidence that you're now working at the same hospital where he's staying," Colin remarks with a nod.

"Even more surprising was hearing his name in Dillon's room when I went to check on him." She takes a sip of water. Colin notices the faint steam rising from her glass—a small, graceful detail that catches his eye, though he can't say why.

Summer continues. "Dillon and his girlfriend both mentioned Fraser's name, and it immediately caught my attention. I don't usually work with coma patients, so it felt a little like fate stepping in."

"Fate stepping in?" Colin repeats softly.

He finds himself genuinely enjoying this unexpected conversation. And inwardly, he wonders, *I meet Fraser's past love on the very day Britney finds her Dillon… could all of this really be fate stepping in?*

— ✦ —

A few days later, Fraser is cleared for discharge from the hospital. As soon as he is out, he calls Colin and asks to meet at a Starbucks.

"Tell me everything that happened while I was in the coma," Fraser requests, eager for details.

Colin recounts the events but deliberately omits the part about meeting and chatting with Summer. He feels it isn't the right time to bring her back into Fraser's life, especially with his family involved.

"You brought Sarah in, and my emotional energy still wasn't enough? Then the next day it suddenly surged enough to wake me up? What could've possibly happened that night?" Fraser asks, pressing for an answer.

But before Colin can respond, a memory stirs — the strange experience Fraser had on the flight back from Philadelphia.

"During the flight, I was listening to some oldies, and a couple of them suddenly made me think of my past girlfriend from ten years ago. It felt so strange."

He glances at Colin. "Colin… was there another woman who visited my room?"

"No. Just the doctors and nurses," Colin replies truthfully. He decides to keep Summer's presence to himself—for now.

213

Shifting the conversation, Colin adds, "Remember the note you left in your SUV about getting some information from Dillon?"

"Oh, I needed to find out what happened to the Gonzalez family before Lucia's accident," Fraser answers immediately.

"When I was in Philadelphia, I noticed that her mind was almost... blank," Fraser continues. "Like she had no emotions left just before the accident. I'm guessing she experienced some kind of trauma that counteracted her positive emotions. If I can figure out what that was, maybe I can help erase that negative feeling and let her emotional energy recover. Hopefully, that can help her wake up."

Colin nods with admiration. "Fraser, you've barely recovered from a coma, and now you're already trying to help another comatose patient? Even Clark Kent wouldn't manage that." He grins, playfully comparing his friend to Superman.

"Clark Kent has his Kryptonite to set him back," Fraser says, looking up with a smile. "I have my family — and you — to push me forward."

Chapter 19 *Tears of an Angel*

The Heartbreak, the Healing, and the Hope

Dillon hands Fraser a report from his interviews with Lucia's daughters and neighbors.

As Fraser reads through it, he learns that Carlos is a loving husband who takes good care of his family. However, a few days before the accident, Carlos had gotten drunk and struck Lucia while the children were watching. He had been under enormous stress after taking out a loan to purchase a counterfeit *'Eyes of an Angel'*—something Lucia had opposed, trying to stop him from wasting money.

"One bruise can black out an entire house of light," Fraser says quietly. "I'm going back to Philadelphia. Now I can help Lucia. The coma taught me how negative emotions block recovery."

Kelsi wraps her arms around his neck. "I know you can do it. You always do. Once you wake her up, we'll make sure she gets a genuine *'Eyes of an Angel'*."

Britney adds softly, "If you can recover from a coma, then anything is possible." Deep down, she knows that courage learns its steps from love—and nothing will stop him from his mission.

Her words carry both tenderness and conviction, echoing the quiet faith they now share.

Fraser looks up gratefully. "I couldn't have done any of this without all of you."

With a playful smile, Britney chimes in, "And thank you, Lord, for Colin's kindness and help in Fritz's recovery. Please bless him with a girlfriend who can keep him company."

She says it gently—an acknowledgment of Colin's unspoken feelings for her, feelings she cannot return.

Fraser takes a flight back to Philadelphia, accompanied by Dillon and Britney. Dillon is excited to show Britney where he has spent his college years, and later, Britney plans to take him to the school where she and her best friend Chloe have made so many memories together.

After five days, Fraser calls Kelsi with excitement.

"Lucia's awake!" Fraser's excitement carries clearly through the phone. "It took days to work through the trauma blocking her emotional responses, but I finally broke through!"

"That's amazing news! When are you coming back? Daniel is learning to talk so fast—you need to be home to see it!" Kelsi responds with equal excitement.

"I need to stay a few more days to ensure Lucia is fully recovered. I also need to teach Carlos how to properly use the *'Eyes of an Angel'*. After that, I plan to visit my alma mater in Pittsburgh for a couple of days. I should be back in seven or eight days," Fraser explains to her in detail, as he usually does.

— ✦ —

Meanwhile, Colin is having dinner with Summer — this time not in the cafeteria but at Tadich Grill in San Francisco. After catching a show at the Orpheum Theatre, they decide to enjoy the long evening together. They've seen each other outside the hospital quite a few times before, but this is the first time they've ended an evening together with dinner.

When the waiter arrives, Colin looks up and says, "Could we have two glasses of hot water, please?"

Summer glances at him, momentarily surprised. "You like to drink hot water too?" she asks. The men she used to know usually didn't.

Colin smiles faintly. "Fraser told me you did. He told me a lot about you."

Just then, the waiter returns and sets two steaming glasses between them.

Her eyes flicker, caught between amusement and memory. The rising steam curls in the air, and for a fleeting instant, she isn't at the restaurant anymore — she's back in that small dorm room years ago, cradling a cup of hot water as Fraser wiped her tears and sang off-key.

Colin's and her eyes meet across the table — the kind of moment that feels both unexpected and inevitable. The soft curl of vapor drifts upward, catching the light like a quiet echo of something unspoken.

Summer wraps her hands around her glass, the warmth seeping into her palms.

"How do you know Fraser?" she asks gently. "You're both so intelligent, yet… so different."

"We both graduated from Carnegie Mellon," Colin replies with a warm smile. "I met him at an alumni party. We share a passion for analyzing brainwaves with AI technology, so it didn't take long for us to become good friends."

"Oh, by the way, is the girl I saw in Dillon's room his sister-in-law? She's so pretty! His wife must be stunning too," Summer comments.

Not entirely sure why women always like to bring up looks in conversation, Colin chooses his words carefully. "Yes, she's very pretty in Fraser's eyes… just as you are very pretty in mine."

He surprises himself with how smoothly the words come out.

Summer's cheeks bloom with a soft blush, and she smiles, waiting to see if he'll say more.

Instead, Colin reaches quietly across the table and gently takes her hands in his. His touch conveys what words might not be able to express.

A couple of weeks later, Colin and Summer are walking along the beach after lunch. When they come across a large rock, Summer sits down and waves Colin over to join her.

"This reminds me of ten years ago when I told Fraser I was going to be engaged," she says with a faint sigh. "I was waiting for his response, but he said nothing. Now I know silence is his answer—though not always the right one."

"But this time, I have something to tell you," Colin says with a mischievous glint in his eyes. "No reruns—this isn't an old scene replayed."

"Then let's rewrite the script together," Summer whispers, her smile trembling between joy and tears. "I have something to tell you too... but I'd rather hear your lines first."

Colin takes her hands. "Jennings offered me a position at U.C. Medical Center. I'd like to accept it—to be closer to you."

Surprised but delighted, Summer grins. "I've applied for a transfer to Stanford Hospital and got approved too. Palo Alto is a much nicer place to live and work than San Francisco," she teases, trying to keep a straight face. "So I guess we'll still have a long commute to see each other..."

They laugh, fingers entwined, pretending to worry about the commute when both already know their hearts are heading to the same home.

— ✦ —

One month later, school is about to start, and Britney is busy reviewing textbooks for her new semester at Stanford. Dillon decides to move his business to the Bay Area, now that the memories of Chloe and Cynthia have been fully replaced by Britney. Meanwhile, Fraser is planning a long cruise vacation with Kelsi, Tiffany, and Daniel, and he has invited Sarah, Jordan, and Audrey to join them. It has been a few weeks since he last spoke with Colin.

When Colin's engagement invitation arrives, Fraser stares at the elegant card. No mention of the bride-to-be's name — typical Colin, always full of surprises.

"Colin's getting engaged? To someone we know?" Fraser asks Kelsi and Britney. "Has he met someone during my coma?"

"Not likely," Kelsi and Britney reply at the same time. "He was so focused on helping you that he barely had time for anything else."

"So he must have met his fiancée recently. It seems like God answered my prayers," Britney reflects, remembering how she prayed for Colin.

"Well, I guess we'll find out at the dinner. I'm really happy for him," Fraser says, giving Britney a thoughtful look.

On the big day, Fraser, Kelsi, Britney, and Dillon all arrive at the restaurant. In the VIP room, they meet Sarah and Jordan. After a brief chat, they settle in, awaiting Colin's arrival.

"Where's your fiancée?" Fraser asks eagerly as soon as Colin walks in.

Colin grins, setting his bag down. "She's nearby," he says lightly. "In fact, Dr. Fraser, she told me you once helped her... in more ways than one." He lets the mystery hang for a moment, clearly enjoying the suspense.

"So Lucia divorced Carlos and married you?" Fraser jabs back, his trademark humor never far behind.

Colin chuckles. "Lucia isn't the only woman you've healed. But before I say more," he adds with a mischievous spark, "let's play Name That Tune. Everyone can look around—but not you." He points playfully at Fraser, who blinks in confusion as the others start whispering and exchanging curious looks.

Colin walks over and gestures toward the door. After a pause, a woman's voice begins to hum the prelude of a nostalgic tune, slow and tender.

Fraser freezes. The sound is so near, yet it feels impossibly far—like a voice from a dream that never quite faded.

Kelsi watches, deeply moved. *"Every time I play that at home, Fritz always goes quiet,"* she murmurs. *"Could this be..."*

The notes continue—gentle, familiar, unbearably close. And then, before he can speak her name, the voice joins in, soft but steady: *"Summertime... and the livin' is easy..."*

Everyone turns toward the entrance. Colin, standing behind Fraser and blocking his view, watches with quiet amusement.

Without realizing it, Fraser begins to sing along, his voice low and trembling: *"Fish are jumpin' and the cotton is high..."* Then, suddenly, he straightens, his voice breaking into a shout. "Summer Tang, is that you?"

Britney and Dillon exchange startled looks as Dr. Tang steps into view. The room falls silent.

Colin steps aside, and Fraser's eyes meet Summer's.

"Summer!" His voice cracks with emotion. "We've been out of touch for years! Even unconscious, I felt you there. How did you find me? How do you know Colin?"

Summer stands at the doorway, smiling softly but saying nothing.

"Say something, Summer!" Fraser pleads again, his voice trembling with eagerness.

She meets his gaze. "It was you who kept silent ten years ago, Fraser," she replies gently. "Now it's my turn." She tries to keep a straight face, but a faint smile betrays her composure.

Fraser takes a step forward, still searching her face. "Then break the silence now," he says softly. "We've lost enough years already."

Summer's eyes glisten; for a moment, she seems ready to answer—but Colin's amused cough cuts through the quiet.

"I think it's time for introductions before someone proposes again," he teases, breaking the tension.

Britney laughs, picking up the cue. "Dr. Tang... I mean, Summer—you're Colin's fiancée?"

Summer laughs lightly. "Guilty as charged. I see Fraser hasn't changed—still dramatic as ever."

"Let the record show that Dr. Summer Tang is hereby found not guilty of all charges," Dillon declares with mock solemnity, "and shall be duly commended in accordance with the Samaritan precedent." He squeezes Britney's hand with a grin. Being an attorney, he's finally learned from Fraser that a well-timed sense of humor can speak louder than any court ruling.

Laughter ripples through the room, easing the air. Fraser shakes his head, smiling. "You can't blame me," he says. "When a ghost from ten years ago starts singing Summertime at my doorstep, I'm allowed a little drama."

"Ghost?" Summer teases, stepping closer. "I'd say more of a delayed miracle."

From the corner, Sarah wipes a quiet tear, her smile soft and knowing. Kelsi catches her glance and returns it, both moved but content to let the moment belong to them.

Colin grins, looking from Fraser to Summer. "All right, you two," he says with a smile, gesturing toward the seats. "Let's sit down before the next verse turns into an opera."

They all sit down at the table, Fraser taking a seat beside Colin.

223

Leaning closer, Fraser asks quietly, "So you knew Summer visited my room. Why didn't you say anything when I asked you?" He knows Colin can't lie.

Colin grins. "I said nobody else came into your room besides doctors and nurses. I wasn't lying." Then, with a deeper smile, he adds, "Your loss is my gain," and begins to share the story of how he and Summer found each other.

As the waiter brings in cocktails, Fraser stands up and raises his glass. "To Summer and Colin—my guardian angels. God works in mysterious ways. While I was trying to help coma patients, He made me one—so I could understand what they need."

"Some lessons need a darkness to be seen." he pauses, his voice filled with emotion. "He knew my family and Sarah weren't quite enough, so He brought Summer back into my life. He made sure I emotionally reconnected with her during my flight through two familiar tunes. He guided Summer to me through Britney and Dillon's conversation. These events are nothing short of a miracle."

With a heartfelt smile, Fraser raises his glass. "But more than that, He brought Colin and Summer together. Let's drink to that, and give glory to our Lord."

The restaurant hums with laughter and clinking glasses. Fraser's gaze drifts. He lets his eyes pass from Kelsi's steadfast grace to Colin's assured pride, from Britney's radiant smile to Dillon's calm resolve, from Sarah's gentle warmth to Jordan's

224

silent courage. Then, almost subconsciously, his gaze lingers on Summer.

At that same instant, she looks up and meets his gaze. As if on cue, they share a silent nod — brief, unspoken, but understood.

How strange, Fraser thought, *that the girl who once broke my heart had returned, not to claim it, but to help heal it.* For a heartbeat, the years fold in on themselves—the girl on the beach, the silence he mistook for strength, the tears he never chased. Yet where pain once stood, now there is something softer. He realized the silence had become something that had pushed him toward faith, toward Kelsi, toward the family that now anchored him.

Summer's presence no longer aches; it blesses. Some loves are not meant to last, but to teach — to carve out space for the love that will. She had once been his unfinished chapter, but tonight he finally turns the page.

His hand finds Kelsi's beneath the table, firm and certain. He doesn't notice Kelsi quietly catching the moment in her heart.

Summer lowers her eyes with a faint smile, then rises and slips toward the terrace. For a fleeting instant, she feels Fraser would follow so they can have a private moment.

But outside, in the cool jasmine-scented air, it is Kelsi's voice that finds her.

"Summer?"

Startled, Summer turns. She still cannot read Fraser's silence—just as before. She offers Kelsi a warm smile, touched with quiet wonder. "Kelsi. I just needed a little quiet."

They stand side by side for a moment, the silence gentle. Then Kelsi speaks, her voice low. "Colin told me someone visited Fraser that night—someone who reached him when we couldn't. Without that…" Her voice falters.

"You don't need to thank me," Summer says gently. "When I heard his name, I couldn't stay away. But I wasn't there to take anything back. I only needed to say goodbye to what never was." To her, closure isn't a door; it's a blessing.

"But…but you saved him." Kelsi stutters.

Summer's eyes glisten. "Maybe I was only the last thread God needed. Some feelings never fade, but the real rope was already braided by you, Britney, the children… and Sarah. I just tied a loose end."

Kelsi blinks back tears. "When Colin said it had to be someone with a deep tie, I was afraid I wasn't enough."

"You are," Summer says firmly. "I saw it the moment I walked in—the unspoken love he shows, the life you've built together. That's love's home. What I felt was only its echo."

Kelsi studies her. "You believe that?"

"I know it. When we reconnected earlier this evening," Summer says, "it felt like he only saw me as a long-lost friend. And when I see the way he looks at you… I realize it's not the love we had — it's deeper, quieter, the kind that stays."

Kelsi feels a small ache rise in her chest, then fades. What she hears isn't comparison — it's truth. Whatever once existed between Fraser and Summer has settled into quiet gratitude, making space for the love that endures.

Their eyes meet. Kelsi whispers, "I'm glad you found Colin."

Summer smiles. "So am I. Fraser and I were young, fiery, but never aligned. Colin and I... we fit. That's grace too."

"Maybe that's how it's meant to be," Kelsi says. "Fraser needed that heartbreak to become the man I love. And you needed it to see what love really looks like."

Summer nods. "God's timing. Always perfect, even when it breaks us first."

The two women embrace, then return inside together.

At the table, Fraser glances up, catching Kelsi's eye; Colin's smile rests on Summer's face. No words pass between them, but the look says everything — gratitude, peace, and a genuine connection more than words can ever explain.

Summer slips into her seat beside Colin, her hand brushing his, and Kelsi takes her place at Fraser's side, fingers still damp from tears but touched by peace.

Fraser lifts his glass again, his voice low but clear.

"I remember, years ago, telling Kelsi about my past. She asked if she might ever meet the woman I once cared about, and I teased that unless she happened to be working at a hospital we visited, that would never happen."

227

Fraser pauses, emotion moving through his voice.

"And yet... God remembered even that small moment. Five years later, He placed me in the very hospital where *she* works — and let her be the one who helped save my life."

He takes a breath, his voice steadying as he looks around the table.

"Some journeys start with invention, others with faith. Mine began with blindness—my own. But through each of you, God teaches me to see. What the mind can't reach, love can. What seems broken can still be made whole. That's the grace of an angel."

His words settle over the table like a quiet benediction. For a moment, even laughter seems to pause to listen. Then glasses rise, and warmth fills the air once more.

The waiter sets down trays of cocktails. Laughter stirs again, soft but bright. Kelsi takes a sip and smiles.

"Funny... it starts a little sharp and bitter, but then it softens and turns sweet. Like love, I guess — it surprises you when it warms up."

"This is a drink Summer and I created," Colin explains. "It's meant to taste like emotions—the ups and downs, the bloom of hope and gratitude."

"This is a nice take, bartender Colin. My AI assistant couldn't have done that. What do you call it?" Fraser teases.

Summer shrugs playfully. "No name yet."

"Tears of an Angel!" Britney blurts, eyes glistening. She sees again the three women—Kelsi, Sarah, and Summer—standing by Fraser's bed, their tears falling onto his face as he opens his eyes shining with life.

For a heartbeat, no one speaks. The name settles over them like a quiet blessing—too perfect to be coincidence, too sacred to taste without tears. Even Colin glances at the glass in silent awe, as if to acknowledge that some moments write themselves.

Glasses lift. Laughter mingles with the clink of crystal. Around the table sit friends, family, loves old and new—all bound together by tears, something deeper than chance.

Fraser looks around once more. Gratitude wells in him—not for angels distant and unseen, but for those seated here, their faces lit by lamplight.

The past has found its place. The future is waiting. Tonight, grace is enough.

Epilogue

Afternoon light filters through the glass walls of a Berkeley computer lab. Fraser sits at his desk, surrounded by open notebooks, circuit boards, and drafts of equations. On one side rests the original *'Eyes of an Angel'* prototype, its lenses catching faint arcs of light. It no longer feels like an invention, but a conversation that never stopped.

Kelsi enters, the children trailing behind, their laughter bright against the low hum of machines. She pauses beside his desk, watching the familiar glow of code on the monitor. "Still working?" she asks, smiling. "What are you building this time?"

Fraser leans back, a glint of quiet excitement in his eyes. "Not building—teaching," he says softly. "An algorithm that helps people see not just what's right in front of them, but what's right within them. Something that guides the heart before the mind decides."

Kelsi tilts her head, intrigued. "Another angel?"

"Maybe," Fraser replies with a smile. "A small one that whispers when the world gets too loud."

She rests her hand on his shoulder. "That sounds like something all of us might need one day."

He glances at the children—playing, laughing, unburdened. "I pray that if they have the hearts of angels," he says softly, "they'll never need it."

The words linger in the light spilling across the desk, illuminating the old prototype beside the new design—two generations of grace, side by side.

Across town at Stanford Hospital, Dr. Colin Stephens finishes his rounds. Dr. Summer Tang stands at the nurses' station, reviewing a patient chart. When she looks up, their eyes meet through the glass wall, a shared smile passing between them— part affection, part gratitude, part remembrance.

"Lunch break?" Colin calls softly.

"Only if you promise not to turn it into a symposium," she teases, gathering her files.

They step outside into the courtyard, where sunlight glints off a bronze plaque near the entrance—one quietly commissioned by a grateful Stanford alumnus whose son was revived by Fraser's modified '*Eyes of an Angel*' device.

The inscription reads:

In Honor of Dr. Fraser Lin — Who Gave Vision to Faith, and Faith to Vision.

Summer pauses, tracing the words with her fingertips. "He never stopped believing," she murmurs.

Colin nods. "He didn't have to," he says gently. "He passed it on."

They stand together in the California light—two healers carrying forward a legacy born not of invention alone, but of love that learned how to see. And somewhere in that brightness, it almost feels as though Fraser's voice still lingers, soft and certain:

"When love becomes your purpose, the rest will always find its way."

೮ೕ ೮ೕ ೮ೕ

᪣ Author's Afterthoughts ᪣

When I started writing this story, it wasn't meant to be a fiction about faith. It began with a simple thought — after reading about how AI was being used to teach a monkey to play video games, I asked myself, *"Why? Isn't using AI to help people heal much more meaningful?"* And so, the first draft was born.

At that time, I didn't even have a name for my story. It began as a quiet thought about how faith, love, and technology can meet at the crossroads of human weakness and hope. It wasn't meant to be a grand idea — only a reflection of how people touch each other's lives in ways science can't quite explain.

But as I continued writing, something shifted — quietly, almost imperceptibly. The story began to lead me instead of the other way around, as if a silent voice was whispering, *"For this to be convincing, you need faith from above."*

Fraser's inventions may come from science, but his journey comes from the heart. The people around him — Kelsi, Sarah, Britney, Colin, Summer, even Jordan and Dillon — each carries a piece of his healing, just as we all carry those who shape us. Some teach us courage. Some remind us what forgiveness looks like. Some leave — and through that leaving, show us what love really means.

Miracles happen in the quiet moments between people who refuse to give up on one another. That's where this story lives.

Kelsi carries the quiet, everyday grace we so often overlook — the kind that stays, listens, and believes when everything else feels uncertain. In her, I see the strength of the woman I share my life with every day. Her love doesn't demand; it endures. And that, to me, is where true healing begins.

Sarah's strength lies in her tenderness. She gives even when her heart is tired, and still loves with a kind of grace that asks for nothing in return. Through her, Fraser learns that love isn't something that needs to be spoken — it's something proven quietly, in patience and care.

And Summer — she is the unforgettable past who once walked through regret, longing, and silence, searching for what time had taken away. Yet even through remorse and distance, she still finds peace under the wings of grace — where memory no longer wounds, but blesses.

Writing this story reminded me that not every love needs to last to matter, and not every miracle comes with bright lights. These moments are quiet ones — the kind that arrive softly, without announcement: a friendship mended, a child's laughter, a prayer whispered in the dark, forgiveness that endures, even a cup of hot water shared between two souls. These are the places where grace took its first breath in this story — the small sacraments of life where heaven quietly touches earth.

Even after writing about miracles and grace, life still finds ways to remind me how imperfectly human I am. One morning at IHOP, I caught myself staring at a plate of waffles, sighing at how simple things could still go wrong — the butter too hard, the waffle too soft, the coffee too light.

Kelsi would have smiled at that — scraped the butter, spread the syrup over my flat waffle, taken my hand, and said, "It's alright, Fritz. The world isn't perfect."

But it's perfect — because that's where it really lives: not in flawless designs, but in a hand reaching across a table, in laughter that softens frustration, in love that turns the most ordinary mornings into blessings — the kind that doesn't change the world, but changes *you*.

If this story has touched you, then maybe grace has done its quiet work again. Because some stories we live only once, yet they ripple through everything we create. And sometimes, the truest loves are the ones that never ask to be named.

— *Francis Leung*

ᚼ Music Acknowledgment ᚼ

Music has always been the quiet pulse beneath the *Angel* stories. Each song named or echoed in *Grace of an Angel* carries an emotion that words alone could never hold—moments of awakening, longing, and the fragile beauty of grace rediscovered.

Lyrics quoted in this novel are the property of their respective copyright holders and are used here for creative and illustrative purposes only.

- *Love Story (Where Do I Begin)* — music by **Francis Lai**, lyrics by **Carl Sigman** (℗ Paramount Pictures / Warner Chappell Music).
- *Do Something* — written and performed by **Matthew West** (℗ Sparrow Records).
- *I Started a Joke* — written by **Barry, Robin, and Maurice Gibb**, performed by **Bee Gees** (℗ Universal Music Group).
- *Summertime* — composed by **George Gershwin**, lyrics by **DuBose Heyward and Ira Gershwin** (℗ Warner Chappell Music).
- *Torn Between Two Lovers* — written by **Peter Yarrow and Phillip Jarrell**, performed by **Mary MacGregor** (℗ Ariola Records).

All rights to these works remain with their respective copyright owners. No commercial use of the lyrics is intended beyond literary reference. Their inclusion here is solely for the purposes in a work of fiction. Each of these timeless songs lent their spirit to remind us that even through heartache, misunderstanding, and change, music remains a vessel of memory, forgiveness, and love renewed.

🕊 About the Author 🕊

Francis Leung is a retired civil engineer with no formal background in literature. He spent much of his career inspecting nuclear power plants, transmission towers, and communication structures — work that required precision, patience, and faith in unseen strength. Never did he imagine that one day he would write fiction.

After retirement, Francis discovered a new way to build — not with steel and concrete, but with words. His stories fuse science with faith and explore how human compassion and divine grace can work together to heal both body and soul.

Grace of an Angel is his first full-length novel, inspired by real experiences and enduring questions of love, hope, and second chances.

Francis serves as a fellowship group leader in his church and finds joy in cooking, baking, and sharing meals with family and friends. He lives in California with his wife and continues to believe that the quiet miracles of everyday life are the most enduring.

🙠 A Glimpse Ahead: Heart of an Angel 🙠

In the next story of the *Angel* series, the miracle of sight turns inward.

When a blind boy and his wheelchair-bound sister discover that true vision begins in the heart, their courage will test the limits of faith, friendship, and love.

Heart of an Angel continues the journey that *Grace* began —where science meets compassion, and the smallest choices can change everything.

www.ingramcontent.com/pod-product-compliance
Lightning Source LLC
Chambersburg PA
CBHW020059180626
46812CB00006B/2389